W9-AWT-117

Camp

of the

Angel

Camp of the Angel

aileen arrington

Philomel Books • New York

for Richard

Copyright © 2003 by Aileen Arrington
All rights reserved. This book, or parts thereof, may not be reproduced in any form
without permission in writing from the publisher,
PHILOMEL BOOKS,
a division of Penguin Putnam Books for Young Readers,
345 Hudson Street, New York, NY 10014.
Philomel Books, Reg. U.S. Pat. & Tm. Off. Published simultaneously in Canada.
Printed in the United States of America.
Designed by Semadar Megged.
Text set in 12.5 point Elegant Garamond.
Library of Congress Cataloging-in-Publication Data
Arrington, Aileen.
Camp of the angel / Aileen Arrington.
p. cm.
Summary: Although teachers, counselors, and social workers try to help, it is
a stray cat that finally enables eleven-year-old Jordan to stand up to the father
who has beaten her and her brother for years.
[1. Family violence—Fiction. 2. Single parent families—Fiction. 3. Schools—Fiction.
4. Cats—Fiction. 5. Islands—South Carolina—Fiction. 6. South Carolina—Fiction.]
I. Title.
PZ7.A743365 Cam 2003
[Fic]—dc21
2002006697

ISBN 0-399-23882-4
1 3 5 7 9 10 8 6 4 2
First Impression

Camp of the Angel

Chapter 1

NONE OF THE OTHERS saw the white cat that day. Just the girl with the dingy plaid dress and the book bag full of homework she had no intention of doing.

The girl didn't even know it was a cat . . . one abandoned, or one of the feral cats, that roamed the island in spells, escaping the eye of the animal control officer. But there it was, waiting behind her house, sunning on the old broken dock above the splashes of green marsh grass as the bus crawled over the bridge to the island, and the girl saw a hint of movement there, something bright white in the afternoon sun.

She strained her eyes to see what it was, but it was too far. A purple windsock whipped in the breeze in back of someone's house. She could smell the sharp, fishy smell off the muddy flats from the river's edge, and the tide rose silently.

The bus moved on to Center Street, and turned to comb the long island roads.

Jordan pushed her dull, dirty blonde hair out of her

face and leaned back, watching out the windows, watching the houses, the summer rental signs, the white crumbled shells in the patches of sand by the side of the road.

School was out and she was happy.

School was where two girls sat and talked about her and acted like they didn't know she could hear.

Well. She did. And she had made up her mind to clean up her yard, too . . . but not because of anything they said. Because of what she *personally* wanted. She had all weekend.

The bus wound around to the back road and whined to a stop. Jordan picked up her book bag and edged down the aisle, looking to see if her little brother was following. She would not look at the ugly yard. She waited for her brother to jump off the bus after her and then she walked straight toward her door.

Inside the old pane glass windows it looked creekwater black, and a lightbulb shone yellow from somewhere back in the house. Behind the door, Jordan glanced to see if Papa was there, to see what mood he was in, and to hide from the school bus that slowly lumbered on down the road.

Chapter 2

IN THE 'FORTIES, THE house had probably been a summer cottage for some well-to-dos who used it to get away from the heat of the city. Then it lay abandoned and neglected and no longer a prize and was bought by Jordan's grandpa nearly forty years ago.

Mama's pa. But Mama left right out of high school and did not return until Grandpa had died. Then Mama came back with Papa and Jordan and Brother to claim her inheritance.

Now the house sat nestled away in a thicket of brambles and myrtles and other untamed growth. Rotting boards that once led to the door lay in a heap, replaced by cinder blocks that Papa found in someone else's yard, someone gone for the winter.

Beyond the brambles, to the back of the house, lay the sparkling tidal river, framed softly with meadows of salt marsh cordgrass and alive with crabs, snails, worms, and birds . . . and tides that rose and fell like long, slow breathing. . . . One time Jordan even saw a porpoise there, strayed in a mile or so down, through the inlet from the open sea.

Jordan's papa was a small wiry-framed man with little steely blue eyes, and rough, red weather-beaten skin. He was employed from time to time, when the mood struck, doing odd jobs for unsuspecting people who summered on the island. But Papa was not often called back, for the work was slow in completion, poorly done, and frequently requiring more material than Papa had planned.

Papa said that Mama had too many secrets. Papa said that Mama would share those secrets with anyone who had half a mind to listen. Papa said the secrets were not real. And it is true that Elizabeth Jordan, as Mama called her, remembered some of this in a vague way, a way that troubled her and made her frown. Elizabeth Jordan didn't like to puzzle over Mama.

Elizabeth Jordan liked to remember the house the way it was when she first saw it. Well-kept. Flowers in the yard. Grandpa's house.

She tried to straighten up after Papa. She always gave up, though, long before she saw any real improvement, finding something better to do with her time. And so the liquor bottles, beer cans, old tires and other junk thrown around the yard collected slowly, as the little house fell sadly under Papa's spell.

Chapter 3

THAT SATURDAY, Jordan went to work on the yard again.

She pitched and lugged the things to the roadside where the trash men would come and cart them off, until Papa hit her hard on the side of her head that Saturday.

"You think this yard's not fancy 'nough for you?" Papa said. He was drunk. His face was red. Jordan felt tears filling her eyes and rage in her heart.

She had been caught off guard one more time. She stared at the grass. She would not look at him. She would never look at him after the beatings. And he never made her.

"You leave my stuff alone," Papa shouted. Jordan said nothing. He never made her speak after the beatings either.

"You understand me?" His words slurred. He stared, breathing hard, and the words stopped. . . . Too tired or dulled to go on.

He didn't want an answer.

Jordan wiped her face, leaving grimy streaks, but no tears for Papa to see. Papa walked away. The screen door slammed.

Jordan slipped back in the woods behind the house to a little hollowed-out place under a thick bush that you could only get to by crawling through tiny tunnels made by rabbits in the underbrush.

A little pair of birds came and lit on a stalk. Tiny birds, brown, the male with a reddish head. Jordan's mama would know their names. Mama knew the names of all the birds. Their songs, too. Mama knew all the birds' songs.

It had been four years since Mama left. Jordan was seven then and too little to learn the songs, but Mama had taught her the mockingbird. The mockingbird sang all the songs and it was a mockingbird that sang to her now.

The bird made her feel better. It was over now, about the yard. She would find Brother, and they would go to the river. She loved the river.

As she started to crawl out, she saw the white cat sitting in the path at the end of the tunnel, a little cat, hardly more than a kitten, and she stopped, sitting back on her heels, surprised. The cat blinked at her with clear green eyes, and Jordan remembered the white thing on the dock she'd seen from the bus and she smiled.

"It was you," she said softly, and Brother called, and the cat ran away.

Chapter 4

WHY DID PAPA hit you?" Brother asked, squinting from behind his thick glasses.

"I was cleaning the yard," Jordan answered.

She looked out across the marsh. A long white bird glided in toward the river, extending his stiltlike legs to meet the water's rippled softness.

" 'Cause you were moving his things?" Brother asked. "Is that why he hit you?"

"Yes," Jordan said.

So now Papa had his yard. Jordan looked down and pushed at an old shell in the mud. An old, old bleached-white shell, lying in the mud among the little fiddler crabs.

"Do you think Mama will ever come back?" Brother asked. The sky was turning golden red to their left, across the bridge, and shooting a glint of sun through the smeary lenses of Brother's glasses.

Jordan knew. Like Brother knew. Mama loved the sunsets.

"I don't know," she said.

"Where do you think she's gone?" Brother asked.

Jordan didn't know. Mama had nerves. Brother knew that, too. Jordan had told him. And the caseworker had stopped bringing Mama to visit.

Papa knew where Mama went. He said he didn't, but surely the caseworker had told him.

"I don't know," Jordan said.

She bent and scooped up the old shell. It was a conch. She stooped to sift the mud off it in the water, wetting her shoes and socks. She stood and held out the shell. "It must be a hundred years old," she said.

Brother came and stared. "You think?" he asked.

"At least," Jordan answered.

"It must be very valuable," Brother said.

"Maybe," Jordan answered. She bent and placed it under a tree.

"You can take it to school," Brother said, frowning. "For show-and-tell."

"We don't have that in my grade," Jordan said. "But you can take it."

Brother picked it up. "Let's take it home."

Jordan considered it. "Papa may not want a shell in the house," she said. "I'll put it in my hideout under the bush. You can get it from there."

A slow boat slipped into view, its motor a soft hum. Jordan watched as the silhouette of the man in the baseball cap and his dog glided by in the boat. She watched the thin, smooth lines spreading behind them on the river. The man waved and the children waved back.

But they did not know the man. Just some man who did not know them. Who did not know their papa. Some man and his dog going to one of the rickety-looking docks that reached out like so many arms from the back of the island.

"We better go," Jordan said, and as she turned, she saw the white cat again lying in the path. Just waiting.

Like it was waiting for them.

They walked over and touched its smooth, silky head, before it bounded away into the brush and out of sight.

Chapter 5

THE SCREENS BILLOWED in the night, in the wind . . . one loose, like a flag, rippling.

On hot nights, Jordan and Brother were allowed to sleep on lawn chairs on the screen porch where there was sometimes a breeze from the water. While the house was small, a cabin really, the porch went the length of it on the river side, though woodsy brush had not been cleared to the dock in years.

Jordan and Brother squeezed into the one old rocking chair together, not yet ready for sleep. The rocker snapped and creaked back and forth against the piping of crickets in the yard.

Gray-blue shadows trailed across the wooden floor planks of the old porch and across their faces, across the bruise on Jordan's forehead. Brother looked at it, his brow knitted in a frown. "Did Papa hit Mama?" he asked.

Jordan shook her head. "No. I don't think so."

Brother turned and looked in the house. It was dark. A light from the television flickered in the hall.

"Monday I get to be All Day Helper at school," Jordan said. "It's gonna be so fun!"

Something moved in the yard. A raccoon maybe, but it was gone now, back toward the marsh. Jordan pushed away the thought that Monday, what with the bruise and all, might not be so much fun. She'd waited a long time for her turn at school, and she wasn't giving it up.

They breathed the scent of wisteria from off to the side of the porch.

"Do you think that cat belongs to someone, Jordie?"

"Maybe some rich people," Jordan decided. "Probably some rich people would have a cat like that."

"Do you think it likes us?" Brother asked.

Jordan felt the night air brush her face. "Yes," she replied. "I think it likes us a lot."

Chapter 6

O N SUNDAY NIGHT, Jordan and Brother had cereal for supper. Papa sat down at the table. He opened a beer and looked at Jordan's face.

"You bruise too easy, girl," he said. They spooned up the cereal. Brother glanced at Jordan.

"What you gonna tell 'em at school?" Papa asked.

"Don't know," Jordan mumbled, swallowing quickly, not knowing the right answer to the question. Not knowing what to say to Papa. Or to say at school.

"What?" Papa yelled. "Don't mumble when you talk to me."

"I don't know," Jordan said. She stared at the plastic contact-paper checks on the table. She stared at the little holes torn open through so much time. From the corner of her eye she could tell that Papa looked scornfully at her face, like he blamed her for it. And then it occurred to Jordan that he did blame her.

It was her fault he had to hit her. It was her fault and she better cover up for it now. Cover up for him because it was her fault.

Brother stared at Papa. "Shut your mouth, boy," Papa said. "You look like a fish." He laughed. Brother shut his mouth and looked back down at his bowl.

Jordan felt the rage again in her heart, and Papa looked into a thin, tiny space in the air that only he could see.

"You kids don't know how good you got it. When I was your age . . ." He didn't finish. They had heard it before.

Papa's papa had been really mean, and it was a wonder that Papa had lived through the beatings he had gotten when he was a boy. But he had learned to respect his old man. That was something kids nowadays did not know about.

Papa got up from the table. He stopped in the doorway. "Jordan can stay out of school," he said. Jordan stared at her food.

Papa went on, "I'll be gone tomorrow before y'all get up. . . . Got a job." He looked at Brother. "But *you'll* be on that bus," he added before he left the room.

Jordan and Brother looked at each other. The cereal was soggy.

"Lucky," Brother whispered. He hated school.

But Jordan didn't know. She had waited and waited and Monday . . . Monday was her turn to be All Day Helper. And sometimes the teacher gave the helper a little prize, too.

So . . . if her bruise faded some more tonight . . .

Chapter 7

JORDAN WENT TO SCHOOL after Papa hit her that Saturday in the yard . . . even after Papa said she could stay out . . . because it was her turn to carry messages and read announcements over the loudspeaker and pass out supplies and lead the line and go get the teacher's things from the office. And Jordan thought no one would see the bruise. Usually the bruises and welts didn't show. The welts would go down and the bruises and little stringy lines of scabs that were left would be covered. But this time Jordan would be careful.

She got on the bus, bending her head forward, so her hair would cover her face. No one would see. She bent over her notebook and made up math problems. No one would notice her face. They wouldn't even notice her.

But they saw her face before the bus got to school.

When she got to class, she tried to cover the colors on her face by leaning her head into her hand.

She stood with the class for the pledge, still tugging on her hair with one hand while putting her other hand over her heart.

While the others went to the library, the teacher kept Jordan in class . . . to help with papers, Jordan thought. It was not for papers though. The teacher wanted to know what happened to Jordan's face. Jordan said she fell.

"Let's go have the nurse look at it," the teacher said, so Jordan went with the teacher to the nurse and the two of them talked, and Jordan told the nurse about falling down and the teacher told the nurse that Jordan told Marsha on the bus that she ran into a door.

Jordan sat in the big, orange plastic chair swinging her feet and holding the ice pack on her face until the counselor came by and Jordan realized she was too old to be swinging her feet like that. She put the ice pack down on the nurse's counter and pulled up her kneesocks, which had slid to her ankles, then picked up the ice pack again. It dribbled a little line of cold water down her arm where she held it. It was made from ice in a plastic Baggie. If she took the Baggie home, she could make herself an ice pack.

Jordan heard the nurse say the school would have to report it. Report what? Jordan thought. Not her. Not her bruise. She hadn't told anything. She whirled around in the chair, clasping the ice pack in her lap and staring into the counselor's office, but now their voices were hushed.

They mustn't report her. Would they get the social workers again to come and talk to her? And to Brother? Like before? Would they come to the house again? And make Papa mad? Not while they were there, but when they left, then Papa would get mad.

It was the law. Jordan remembered that they said it was the law about reporting it. And it was the law about visiting within twenty-four hours and then they went away and *you* stayed. Jordan knew about the law.

Chapter 8

J ORDAN WAS SENT TO the library and later that day they called for her over the speaker and she went to the counselor's room with the lamps and the teddy bears and all the books about problems children have and a little tank of pretty fish that she liked to watch.

"You must like aquariums," the counselor said.

Jordan nodded. They were the most beautiful fish she had ever seen. They were more beautiful than she could have imagined. If she had a tank of those fish she could sit and look at them for hours and hours.

"Did you bring them from home?" Jordan wanted to know.

"No," said the counselor. "These stay here."

Jordan was delighted. Her eyes glistened as she watched the fish swim in their clear little tank with the water bubbles and the pretty pastel shells and the turquoise-blue pebbles and tiny green plants.

"What are the bubbles for?" Jordan asked, bending over to look more closely.

The counselor didn't know why her pretty little fish

needed the bubbles in the tank, and Jordan thought if she ever got a tank of fish like that, she'd sure find out what the bubbles were for.

She offered to look it up for the counselor in the library. The counselor said she'd like that and she thought maybe Jordan could get out of class sometime and help her clean the tank.

"Would you like that?" she asked.

Jordan said she would like that a lot.

"But why don't you take them home?" Jordan asked. She could not imagine having something so wonderful and not taking it home. Unless . . . Well, she couldn't imagine being the counselor and not taking them home.

"I have a bigger aquarium at home," the counselor said.

"Oh." Jordan's eyes were bright.

"But these are for you students," the counselor continued.

The counselor was really nice, Jordan thought, except for being so nosy. Other than that, she was real nice.

"How are things with you, Jordan? At school? At home?"

But Jordan didn't want to talk about that. She leaned over on her folded arms and stared in the tank.

"They're like jewels, only alive," Jordan said.

When the social worker arrived, the counselor told Jordan to come sit down. Jordan sat in a big, overstuffed easy chair. She talked to the counselor and the social worker and the principal and she told them about the way she fell down *and* ran into a door.

The social worker wrote something in a folder and Jordan sat up, trying to see, but she could not.

Chapter 9

JORDAN WENT AND WAITED again in the clinic. She asked the nurse for another ice pack. She would save it with the other Baggie in her book bag back in the room.

Brother came and sat beside her in the big plastic chairs.

"Have they talked to you, too?" Brother asked.

Jordan looked at him. "Yes," she said.

Both pairs of feet swung above the green tile of the floor.

"What did you say?" Jordan whispered to Brother so the nurse would not hear. Brother had told a different story.

"I said you got knocked down on the cinder blocks by that big dog that comes around," Brother whispered. His eyes were worried behind the glasses. Jordan did not reply. She put the ice pack back on her face. Though her face was numb with cold right now, maybe the ice would make the bruises go away if she kept it there. And then they would not have to come and see Papa.

"Did you say that, too?" Brother asked, but his face showed that he knew enough to know she had not. And his face began to crumple.

"It's okay," Jordan whispered. "I should have told you what to say. Next time we'll know." She put her arm around her little brother's shoulders. "Don't cry. We don't want them to see us cry," Jordan whispered. "Did you see the fish?"

Brother sniffled and stopped crying. "Yes," he said.

"Aren't they beautiful?" Jordan said. They sat in the tall plastic chairs with the silver-colored legs and swung their feet and thought about the counselor's bright-colored little fish in the clear sparkling tank, and waited.

"Do you think we could catch some like that back of the house?" Brother asked. The nurse looked up at them and smiled and Jordan stopped swinging her feet again. The nurse went back to the papers she was filling out.

"I never saw any," Jordan said.

Brother said, "I know where there're some old nets."

Jordan looked toward the closed door to the counselor's office. She thought of the crystal-clean little tank of shiny fish.

She'd seen mud minnows in the marsh.

Her eyes brightened and she looked at Brother.

"After school today," she said.

The social worker called them back in and told them that she would be coming to their house and asked would their dad be there this afternoon.

"No," Jordan said, suddenly relieved. "He's on a job. And he's always late when he's on a job."

There was no reason now for the social worker to come.

"I need to take a picture of your face," the social worker said.

Jordan looked around the counselor's office at the big plants on the window sill and the pretty rug on the floor and some photographs of children from the school tacked on a little bulletin board with calico cloth for borders. Not photos like the one that would be taken of her. And they would not put her picture there.

Jordan looked at the social worker. She didn't want her to do this, but didn't think she could stop it. The social worker got out her camera and Jordan pushed her fingers through her hair and smiled slightly. The camera flashed, the picture came out of the bottom, and the social worker put it in her file.

Brother went back to class and Jordan stayed for another ice pack because hers lay melted on the nurse's counter by then, and she heard the social worker tell the counselor that Jordan's dad was skipping something called anger management classes.

Papa never told them about that. Perhaps, Jordan thought, it was because he was ashamed for them to know. Ashamed the social workers could tell him to go.

Perhaps Papa was ashamed, too, of his anger.

Chapter 10

APPARENTLY THE SOCIAL worker was not sure that Papa wouldn't be there after school. She took Jordan and Brother home that day, and they saw the white cat sitting on top of a closed trash can just past where the pavement ended at the end of their street. It jumped off and ran down a sandy dirt road into the woods as the car approached.

"Did you see that pretty cat?" Jordan asked.

"It was pretty," the social worker said. "I'll bet she's hungry, poor thing, and looking for food in that garbage."

"That cat comes around our house sometimes," Jordan said. She twisted her neck back to look for it as they turned in her driveway.

Papa was not there.

"He's gone," Jordan said.

The social worker went to the door anyway.

"I can tell you whatever you want to ask him," Jordan said, following the social worker back to her car, but the social worker said she would be back. Jordan and Brother stood in the yard and watched her drive away. They went to the kitchen and got sodas to drink. They knew the social worker had her mind made up.

They waited in the hideout that afternoon and they heard Papa's car come home and they heard the social worker's car come back again. They waited until they thought they heard the car leave. And then they waited some more.

Jordan wished that they could go somewhere and not ever have to go in that house. She looked at Brother. He was rocking back and forth in little choppy movements.

"We gotta go now," she said. "But he won't whip us. Not now. Not when they just came and they'll be asking us stuff at school."

Brother pushed his dark-rimmed glasses up on his nose.

They crawled out from the little hollow and walked back to the house. They could hear the television going when they went in the back to the kitchen. They stopped and looked at each other. It was getting dark in the house. Jordan swallowed hard. She walked to the living room. Papa glared at her as she stood in the opening, Brother behind her.

"Should I go and make our supper?" she asked. She tried to sound normal.

The television played an old black-and-white show. It was a show Jordan liked. It was funny. It didn't belong here though. Not now.

Papa said, "You call the shots . . . huh? Is that the way it works now?"

"No," Jordan said. She studied the markings in the floorboards. Markings that looked like some kind of face . . . like a Halloween-mask face.

"I tell you to stay out, but you march down there anyway 'cause you wanna run your big mouth."

Jordan shook her head no.

"But you know what the problem is?" Papa said. "You don't tell anybody the truth."

Jordan stared at the face in the floor . . . at the mouth like an O.

"Buttinsky and her bleeding hearts, they'll believe anything you tell 'em. . . . And you know it, don't you? . . . Huh, Jordan?"

"No, Papa, we tried to tell them it was an accident." Jordan scrunched her eyebrows together. The face in the floorboards watched her.

"You want to tell me why they come out here over an *accident?*" Papa yelled. He took a swallow from his beer.

"I told them I fell down," Jordan said in a little voice.

"And Carson done told them another damn story," Papa yelled. "Get your face out here, boy!" Brother moved beside Jordan. "Stupid. Two stupid kids. You two are really something, aren't you?" Another swallow from the can.

Jordan and Brother hung their heads. Papa glared.

"I'll go make our supper, if you want me to. I'll do that now," Jordan said, backing out of the room and Papa looked back at the television.

Jordan left the light off in the kitchen. It might make Papa mad if they turned it on, wasting it, when it was light enough to see.

She went to the cabinet and got out two bowls and the cereal. Brother poured it. Jordan got the milk. They ate in silence, shoveling it down, watching the door, making themselves eat. They weren't hungry now, but they would be hungry later if they didn't eat. They went and sat on the back steps.

"It's warm now," Brother said. "It's like summer."

They listened as the quiet sounds of the island settled in toward nighttime. Clear sweet calls from the woods and beyond. An occasional solitary car passing by out front of the house. Someone heading home, some stranger, perhaps the man with the cap, someone who didn't know Jordan and Brother. Someone who didn't know Papa and the social worker.

Someone who did not know.

Late April had been cooler than usual this year, though the spring flowers had come out, the air had been cool. The yellow flowers that grew wild dipped in the warm breeze. Brother was right. It was warm now. But Jordan shivered.

"Perhaps Papa will take us to fish tomorrow," Brother

said. He pushed at his straggly hair. "It would be good to go to the creek, wouldn't it, Jordie?" he said.

Jordan kept her eyes on the flowers. She rubbed her skinny arms with her hands. "It'd be good," she agreed.

"Do you think we'll go tomorrow?" Brother asked.

"Soon," Jordan said, "but not tomorrow. Tomorrow we gotta go to school. If we don't, they'll be asking questions."

She put her hand to her face.

Tonight when Papa was watching television, she would get ice and put it in the Baggies from school. She would keep it on her face in bed. In the morning, maybe the colors would be gone.

And some other day, some day when she hadn't got them in such a mess, then they'd try to find some tiny fish, and put them in a pretty jar to look at, and maybe even that white cat would want to come around and look at some tiny fish in a jar, too.

Jordan watched the deep yellow of the flowers bobbing in the darkening light of the day. The colors would go away, and they would search for tiny fish. One day soon.

Chapter 11

WHEN THE WEATHER was warm Papa would take Jordan and Brother with him to fish and crab in the tidal creeks, sometimes just off the road to town so the bus would ride by and the island children would tell Miss Field that Jordan and Carson were down by the creek fishing with their daddy again, instead of being in school where they belonged. And the teacher would ask Jordan if she had a note for being absent from school and Jordan would say no. And the attendance clerk would send home a letter explaining the law again, about absences, and Jordan would ask Papa to write her a note because she didn't want to be kept back in school for unexcused absences.

And now Papa had kept them out. Right after the social worker, Jordan thought. Sort of like to show them who's really in charge.

Jordan was embarrassed to go back to school, and glad to stay out, because Papa wasn't mad anymore, and it was easy for Jordan to think Papa liked her and Brother when he was not mad. It would be a good day.

That morning Jordan and Brother went with Papa fishing, out behind someone's summer house near the back of their lot.

"Belongs to the Vanderbilts," Papa said about the place. It was a name Papa had for rich people. Jordan and Brother laughed.

They ran ahead through the path to the people's backyard and down the long wooden boardwalk over the marshes. They climbed down to the floating dock on the water. Their feet made hollow metal sounds on the ramp.

They watched a bird snapping for lunch in the water back by the tall cordgrass, its feathers white, its thin black legs picking through the shallows, and Papa fished in the river.

This was where Mama had taught Jordan and Brother to swim one spring when they were very small. Mama had said the people there never came except in the summer, and Mama knew those people, too, when she was a girl. So it was all right to use their dock. They would not mind.

Jordan and Brother asked Papa if they could swim today.

Papa laughed. " 'S fine with me if you wanna get in there with them eels," he said.

Jordan was not afraid of eels. "Just skinny fish," she laughed, and jumped in.

The water surrounded her, soft and cool and wet and deep at the high tide, to where she did not touch the bottom. She bobbed to the surface, her hair all flat and wet and clinging to her neck, her face covered with beads of salt water.

"What you waiting for?" she yelled at Brother, and he cannonballed off the side of the dock.

Papa gathered up his things. "Gotta meet a man about some money," he said, and left them to play in the water. "Watch out for the varmits!"

Jordan and Brother laughed. Papa could be real funny when he wanted.

The river was cold and the sun warm. They wore shoes. Oyster beds on the bottom could cut bare feet, so they swam in their shorts and T-shirts, and their heavy-with-water sneakers, dog paddling out deeper in the blue salty water, laughing and shouting at the cold and the fun of being in that water, choppy with little waves made by the wind and the incoming tide.

When they got hungry for lunch, they climbed out, dripping and laughing at the soaked shoes that squished out water and made wet splashy tracks all the way back on the boardwalk.

At the house, a blue pickup truck with peeling paint was pulling out of the driveway. The man at the wheel looked none too friendly, but Papa seemed okay.

Jordan sat on the front steps, enjoying drying in the sun. She was filled with a sense of summer coming . . . warm weather and lots of time outdoors . . . maybe even a few more swims before the Vanderbilts came to their extra house. Today had been like a vacation. A little vacation all in itself.

Chapter 12

THE NEXT MORNING Jordan asked Papa for excuses for her and Brother to take to school.

Papa laughed and said, "What should I write? 'Jordan and Carson were out of school because they wanted to go fishing with their daddy'?" and Papa laughed again, but after he had his fun, he wrote a note that he had to keep them home " 'cause they were sick," and Jordan knew that the teacher would know it was a lie, but maybe she wouldn't tell the attendance clerk, and maybe the principal wouldn't find out. Or the guidance counselor.

The guidance counselor is how Jordan found out where Mama was.

Jordan and Brother took the notes to school. Jordan's note said she could take an aspirin if she wanted it. Jordan told Papa to put that in, even though she wouldn't need an aspirin. And Papa was nice to put that in the note for her, because now she could spend time out of class taking the aspirin.

The people at school wondered what Jordan and Brother were both out of school with yesterday.

"Sore throats," Jordan said.

It was what she had told Brother to say, too. This time they had their stories straight.

Jordan stood fingering her aspirin in her pocket. "Papa said it might be strep throat," she said. "So, just to be on the safe side, we had to stay out."

Jordan saw the teacher look at the counselor and the nurse. The teacher didn't believe it.

"We were running fevers, too," Jordan said. "We were both a hundred."

Jordan didn't know anything else to tell them. She stooped and licked her fingers to clean her dirty sneakers.

Maybe she was saying too much. Like Mama. Talked too much, Papa said.

Perhaps, Jordan thought, I am too much like Mama was. . . .

Chapter 13

MAMA WAS A REAL nervous person. That's why she used to talk so much. Before she got her nerves under control better.

Jordan had figured this out about Mama a couple of years ago. She had figured it out the way she wanted it to be.

Jordan figured there was nothing much really wrong with Mama. Just nerves. That was all. After the caseworker had told Jordan Mama had a brain disorder, Jordan had looked it up at school. Brain. Nervous system. Same thing.

Mama had nerves. Mama's brain disorder was nerves.

Around the time Jordan figured it out, when she was nine and Brother was six, they went on a visit with Mama to a little park with lots of flowers. Brother had told Mama that Papa said Mama was crazy, and Mama had said no. She was not.

Jordan and Brother knew that Papa said bad things

about Mama. Things that did not have to be true. They knew Papa did not like Mama anymore.

The caseworker had said that crazy was a rude word. And that Mama could have done something, because of her disorder, that seemed crazy to Papa.

Jordan thought about what the caseworker said.

Seeming crazy is not *being* crazy, Jordan told herself.

So when the caseworker asked Jordan that time if she had any questions about Papa saying that about Mama, Jordan said no. Because Jordan liked the way she had it figured out.

From then on, Jordan did not ask any Mama questions, and later when the caseworker told Jordan the name of Mama's disorder, Jordan did not look it up.

Chapter 14

THERE WAS NOT TOO much the teacher and the counselor could do about finding out if Jordan and Brother both really had sore throats the day after the social worker's visit. So they gave up, and Jordan stopped at the nurse's desk just outside the counselor's door to ask for one of the pretty little paper cups to take her aspirin with. Jordan liked the paper cups and the nurse was very generous with her supplies. Jordan liked the nurse.

While Jordan was waiting for the cup, right outside the counselor's door, she heard the counselor say to someone that Jordan's mama was back on Bull Street.

When Jordan first heard it, she didn't think anything. She knew Mama had lived different places since she left.

So when she heard the counselor say that, it occurred to Jordan that Mama was settling back in another house.

That night, as Jordan washed dishes, the words came back to her about Mama being on Bull Street, and from somewhere in her experience it came to her that that was where the state hospital was. Up in Columbia on Bull Street. Bull Street was where they sent crazy people.

Jordan put the last plate in the drain basket and stood watching drips of water fall from the plate into the plastic tray and run over the side into the old porcelain sink.

When Jordan thought about what the counselor had said about Mama, what it meant, it did not really surprise her.

Somehow she had already known.

Chapter 15

THAT NIGHT A FAINT smell of salt drifted off the river on air that was warm and cool at the same time and Jordan came to sit by Brother on the back steps. They put their hands on their knees and stared up into the lace of the live oak's thousands of tiny leaves.

"Why'd Papa say the cat was ugly?" Brother asked.

Jordan folded her arms tightly to her. She felt the stirrings of anger. She had told Papa at supper about the pretty cat they saw, and Papa had said he saw an ugly white cat out at the garbage can. "Probably the same thing," he had said, and laughed.

"I don't know why," Jordan answered. "Cats are not ugly." She frowned.

The sky was dark blue against the wind-shaped myrtles toward the river, and a whisper rustled in the leaves above.

"I went to the dock," Brother said. "It wasn't there."

"It's probably home," Jordan said. "It probably went home for supper and now it's asleep."

But something didn't set right. That wasn't the first time the cat was at a garbage can. "Let's feed that cat," she said. "Maybe it's not getting enough food."

She sunk her toes into the sand at the bottom of the steps. She felt better. The island was quiet. Like an angel's camp. It was a good place for an angel to camp.

Mama said an angel of the Lord would make a camp around people. People that fear the Lord. It was in the Bible.

When Jordan was little, she thought perhaps the angel's camp was down one of the little sandy roads that trailed away through the trees here and there on the island. Because you could not see down those roads. You couldn't see what was down those roads. Maybe the angel.

Chapter 16

AROUND THE TIME Jordan saw the white cat, Papa took to spending more time away from the house. Papa would go out after supper and Jordan and Brother would stay by themselves. They would watch movies on television and go to bed when they got sleepy.

Sometime later at night they would hear Papa come home. Sometimes Papa would bring friends home. Loud men and women who laughed and cursed and drank a lot. On those nights Jordan would pull her thin blanket up high to her chin, her ears keen to pick up on every sound, alert until the noises stopped, until the friends were gone.

Brother slept in a small bed on the far side of Jordan's room. Jordan's bed, a huge rusted metal frame with squeaky coil springs under the lumpy mattress, seemed not a small enough place to hide. Sometimes Jordan would slip out of her bed and scurry over to wait by Brother in his small wooden-framed bed. Brother would be lying on his back staring with wide eyes through his thick lenses.

Brother always got his glasses and put them on when the noise from Papa and his friends woke them. The two watched the door, which was always open. Papa didn't allow them to ever close the door. So the yellow light would stream in and spill over Jordan's bed. But here in Brother's corner no light fell. And so they would watch the door and listen to the sounds and wait.

When the friends were gone, Jordan would creep back to her bed and Brother would put his glasses back on the table and they would still watch until sleep came and morning came, too soon.

Chapter 17

JORDAN WAS USING THE white pastel crayon and pushing down as hard as she could on the paper to make her picture of the white cat look just right when Brother's teacher came to the door of the trailer where art class was held. She came to talk to Jordan.

Was everything all right at home?

"Yes."

Was there anything Jordan needed to let her know about?

"No."

The teacher wanted to talk to her about Brother. He was causing trouble again. Once he'd gotten detention. And a beating from Papa, too.

"Carson has been hitting the other children," the teacher said. "I really need to talk to your father. Do you have a phone?"

"It's cut off," Jordan said, but she would tell Papa, and he would surely stop Brother from ever doing that again. Jordan shifted from one foot to the other. She squinted up at Mrs. Evans. She wanted to go back in and finish her picture.

"Carson is sleeping in class, too. When did he get to sleep last night?"

"After supper," Jordan said, "but there were people over to the house. They made a lot of noise." Jordan tightened her lips and stared at the basketball court.

The sounds came back to her now . . . from her yard. A man's voice. A voice she did not know. "I'll get 'er." A crashing sound of a beer can thrown, hitting the garbage pail. Laughing. Was it the white cat? Was he throwing at the white cat? At any cat? She had laid there in her bed and hoped he had missed.

"Does your father have a work phone?"

"He works for different people, painting and stuff," Jordan said.

"What about your mother?" Mrs. Evans asked. "Maybe I need to talk with her."

"We don't see her much," Jordan said.

Mrs. Evans wanted to know when did they see her and Jordan said Mama's caseworker took them places to visit with Mama. Nice places. Papa would not be around Mama. Papa had divorced Mama. But sometimes he would let Brother and her go with the caseworker and Mama to a park, or to the mall, or to Chuck E. Cheese's or the ice-cream store.

Brother's teacher smiled at Jordan. "Well, that sounds

nice, Jordan," she said. "Those are fun places to go. And you tell your daddy what I said." She paused and studied Jordan. "You seem like a very nice girl, Jordan. I just wonder if maybe you could talk to your brother also about not hitting the other children. Would you do that for me? And then maybe I won't need to talk to your daddy."

Jordan smiled back. A soft rushing sound came from high in the pines. "I'll do that," she said.

"All right then . . . and I'll talk to Carson some more myself . . . and we'll see. Okay?"

Jordan nodded and smiled. Mrs. Evans was nice.

Jordan went back to her drawing. It had been a week since she'd seen the cat. And she wanted to feed it. She smoothed the white pastel with her finger. It was not pretty as she would like. It was not pretty as the white cat. But it was good.

On the bus after school Brother would not talk. He would only look at the floor. A girl from Brother's room told Jordan that Brother had gotten a detention but the teacher had taken it back and just given him twelve sentences to write.

I will not hit other students.

"That's good that you don't have the detention, isn't it?" Jordan said. Brother still wouldn't talk. "And I'll help you with the sentences," Jordan added. Brother looked at Jordan.

Jordan showed him the picture she drew in art class

of the white cat. She said he could have it. He took it and studied it. A girl and a boy and a white cat.

The next day Jordan and Brother went to Brother's room before school. Brother took his twelve sentences to Mrs. Evans. And he took the picture Jordan drew of the white cat to show to Mrs. Evans. Brother told Mrs. Evans that the cat was his. His and Jordan's.

Mrs. Evans said they surely had a very pretty cat and Mrs. Evans said since they liked animals she had something for them.

Jordan and Brother watched wide-eyed as the teacher went to her cabinet at the back of the room.

The sun was just reaching in through the schoolhouse window and painting squares of light onto the floor. Mrs. Evans brought out two brand-new little boxes wrapped in cellophane. The boxes were from animal charities and were full of colorful picture postcards and note cards with different animals on each one.

"These people send me so many of these I can't use them all. So I bring them to school to give to my students. Would you like them?" Mrs. Evans held out the boxes.

Jordan and Brother looked at the boxes and beamed. They nodded and the boxes were theirs.

On the way home in the bus, Jordan read Brother what it said on each card about the animals, and they admired the pictures. They stuck some of the cards on the mirror in their room at home. They picked out one each to give to Mama the next time they saw her. And they tucked the others away in the top drawer.

"To mail to someone," Jordan said, though she did not know, when she said it, who they would mail them to.

Chapter 18

P APA WAS ANGRY. THE night he got mad about the cornflakes, he'd come home angry. He walked in the front door and Brother jumped up out of Papa's chair and Papa sat down, tired and cursing. Jordan sat still where she was on the sofa. Brother slipped down beside her and they both stared at the television, no longer interested in the show.

"The hell with him," Papa growled. "Let him get some college boy to do the damn job. See if he likes the work then. . . . "

Papa had gone to ask for work from the real estate man, the one who handled the summer rental houses. The one who had given him work before. Papa needed money for the taxes on the house and on the property. Papa had always had the money before. Papa had always bragged to his friends about the way he paid no rent, just the taxes once a year, but no rent. And it was a good deal not to have to pay rent because Mama owned the house, because Grandpa had the house all paid for when he died.

But now Papa did not have the money for the taxes. And now the real estate man would give no work to Papa. Papa's eyes were hard and cold as he looked over at Jordan. "Bring me a beer."

Jordan went to get it from the kitchen. Papa drank and got quiet, sullen. Jordan and Brother remained on the couch, afraid to leave, afraid Papa wouldn't like it if they left, wanting to leave, and then Papa told them how he had gone in the little real estate building real friendly and asked if there was any work he could do and the girl said she didn't know of any. Papa asked to talk to the owner and he came out and said the same thing, that there was no work right then and that he had someone who would be doing most of his work, and Papa even explained he was a little short right now, with the property tax due but the man shook his head and said he didn't have anything.

"Treats you like y' ain't nothin'," Papa said. "Nothin'. Makes you beg and then looks down his nose and says no."

Jordan had felt sorry for Papa then. The man was mean.

Papa called someone named Jim and said he was short of cash and was thinking about what Jim had said. "Yeah," Papa said. "Call me. We'll set up a time to talk."

"You got a job now?" Brother asked. Jordan thought Papa might get mad at Brother for asking that, but Papa just said "Yeah."

Jordan looked at Papa. It was funny. If Papa could get a job that quick, why was he mad at the real estate place?

Later that night Papa got mad about the cornflakes, about Jordan wasting the cornflakes, and about Brother not appreciating the cornflakes and wanting frosted flakes instead and being spoiled. And then Jordan didn't feel sorry for Papa when he beat them.

Chapter 19

T HE NEXT MORNING was Saturday and Papa took Jordan and Brother to the ocean on the eastern side of the island. He took them to the rocks that protruded into the tide pools. They walked the six quiet blocks of old bungalows and cabins and carried buckets and nets on the ends of poles to catch crabs by the rocks.

Jordan stood on the warm sand under a blue sky at the edge of the clear, foaming salt water.

"When can we come here and swim, Papa?" she asked.

Papa stopped poking around in the water. The wind whipped at Jordan's hair.

Papa turned and stared at her coolly. "You know how to swim in an undertow?" he asked.

"No, sir," Jordan answered, afraid to break her glance away from him once he had caught her eye.

"Then don't go asking stupid questions."

Jordan looked to where Brother was sitting on the sand taking off his shoes and socks. She glanced back at Papa.

"What are you planning on doing?" Papa shouted into the wind at Brother. Brother froze with his sock halfway pulled off.

"Wading," Brother said.

"Put those shoes back on!" Papa said.

The gulls called and the waves sizzled and after each wave slipped back to meet the ocean, tiny fountains of salt water would gush up from little holes in the wet sand. Jordan hoped they would come here again.

There was not much to catch that day, or their luck was bad, and Papa would not be going back.

As they carried the poles and buckets in the shade at the edge of the blacktop on the way back to the house, Jordan and Brother asked Papa if they could walk down to the ocean some other time. And they asked Papa if he would take them to the fishing pier. They had never been out on the pier.

"You don't need to go there," Papa said. And though they were sometimes allowed to walk to the Laundromat or to the convenience store to get something for Papa, they were forbidden to go anywhere else on the island.

Papa was angry. He walked fast. Brother started to ask another question, and Papa stopped in the road.

"Look here," he said. "My time's wasted enough 'cause of the two of you . . . getting that woman on my case . . . so just shut up with y' whining."

The sun grew hot when they moved out of the shade. Jordan lagged behind watching Papa. The anger classes.

Maybe Papa had to go there later this afternoon and that's why he was mad. Jordan was sorry. She would much rather have Papa take them to the pier.

Brother was lugging a bucket of dripping grainy beach sand to play with. She should have brought one herself . . . to make a sand castle in the driveway.

The wind picked up and rattled softly in the palmettos, rattled the dried fronds hanging in the palmettos, and then Jordan saw the white cat. It lay licking its fur in a patch of sun down the sandy dirt road.

"Hey, little cat," Jordan called softly. The cat lifted its head and watched her.

"What you doin' back there, girl?"

"Nothing, Papa," Jordan said, and hurried to catch up.

"Who you talking to back there?"

"Nobody, Papa," Jordan said.

Papa looked at her. A girl talking to nobody. She could tell what he thought before he looked away.

Papa thinks I am like Mama.

Chapter 20

PAPA TOOK JORDAN and Brother to the store for lunch. He bought them hot dogs. He stayed in the store while they went outside and Jordan tore off part of her hot dog meat. "We'll have it if the white cat comes this afternoon," she said to Brother, and he grinned and pinched off some of his and handed it to Jordan. She wrapped the pieces in a napkin and hid it in her pocket.

They went to eat their lunches on a picnic table over by an ice truck parked by the side of the little white cinder block store.

"Why do you think Papa doesn't like the ocean?" Brother asked.

Jordan looked at the blue neon letters in the window of the little store. ICE HOUSE it said. She looked at the hand-lettered fish bait sign. "Maybe he doesn't know how to swim," Jordan said. "Maybe he's afraid."

"That water looked so cool and bubbly," Brother said. "I wish he'd let us go in that water." He took off his glasses and wiped them on his shirttail. He opened his bag of potato chips.

" 'Member when we used to go to the ocean with Mama?" He squinted at her through the scratched lenses.

Jordan looked across a vacant lot, past a tiny house and a giant blue umbrella, to the dunes, to the ocean there, showing just a little between an ancient tumble-down inn and a new apartment house.

"I remember," she said.

Chapter 21

WHEN JORDAN moved to the island, Mama would often take her and Brother and they would walk to the ocean, sun splashed and green with dark blue shadows from the clouds above, dark blue shadows that flowed like the water. And breakers, long and soft and white.

Sometimes they would walk all the way to the churning water at the northern inlet and look at the lighthouse out in the sea.

"Tell us about the lighthouse man," Jordan would say, because Mama would always have a story about a man who had a boat that was like a big, big seashell and the boat would dance across the waves and the man called it the *Shell Dancer*. And the man would go out in the *Shell Dancer* in that water to the lighthouse.

Mama would look and look at the lighthouse and Mama said she went out there to that old lighthouse many times in the man's boat.

Jordan had asked Mama one time if they could go there in the man's boat, and Mama said she saw that man with his boat that very morning at the post office, and when she saw him again she would ask him.

That day they had forgotten to take food or leave in time for lunch and they got very hungry and had a long walk back to the house. Brother cried and wanted to be carried, and Mama did carry him even though he was four or five years old then and too old to be carried, because Mama wanted to shush him because all the noises were getting too loud for Mama on that walk back to the house.

They moved off the beach to the road but the noises were still there for Mama. Jordan had not understood why Mama could hear the loud noises and she could not. The island was quiet. Few cars passed them. An occasional gull. The sound of the surf, hushed at low tide.

Jordan had looked around and looked at Mama and not understood, and even now Jordan did not like to wonder what it was that Mama heard that day.

After that, the noises bothered Mama more and more and Mama never did see the lighthouse man again to ask him if he would take them out in the inlet in his boat.

When Mama left, Papa had packed up all her things and sent them away. Everything of Mama's was gone. Even the stories. When Mama left, Jordan realized that Papa was right. Jordan could not tell what was real of what Mama had said. And so she stopped thinking about the stories.

Chapter 22

PAPA LEFT. THE AFTERNOON wore on. The little house stood quiet in the dusky gray shadows and the sun was soft and gold, high in the oaks, and out toward the river. Jordan and Brother found the hot dogs they saved for the white cat in the refrigerator, and went down the little woodsy path to what was left of the old dock. No more than nine feet before the boards were gone, taken out long ago by a hurricane and never replaced. The posts were left alone, to trail far into the tall grasses and on out to the choppy blue moving water of the river. Jordan and Brother stood and watched. From time to time, they looked toward the woods and at other docks in the distance that reached across the acres of marsh, but there was no flash of white that would be the cat.

"What if she won't come here today?" Brother asked.

Jordan glanced at the bag with the hot dogs waiting on the dock. "We can save more food. Another day," she said, not wanting to wait for another day.

After a while Brother said, "I know where there's a big old jar."

"An aquarium!" Jordan said. "For tiny fish!"

Brother ran off and came back with a big pickle jar, and the nets from that morning.

They waded into the water and stood, searching with their eyes, searching between the cordgrasses and under the dock.

Brother whacked the water with his pole net. "I saw some!" he yelled.

Jordan laughed. "You scared them away!"

Brother raised his net over his head and grinned. They chased another school of little gray fish with the nets, but the fish were too fast that day. They splashed each other with the nets on the water and laughed loud enough to think they'd scared all the fish away, so they climbed up on the dock and took off their wet sneakers and lay on their bellies staring over the edge of the dock for more fish.

Something made them turn. The white cat was on the dock.

Jordan and Brother glanced at each other. Jordan put her finger up. Brother nodded. "I know. We won't scare her," he whispered. They fed the cat. They put pieces of meat on the dock and she came and ate. She cleaned her fur. They wished they had saved more hot dog. The sun dropped lower and across the river little telephone poles leaned slightly this way and that against a pale yellow sky. The white cat settled for a nap just out of reach. Jordan and Brother sat cross-legged and watched, not wanting to break the spell.

Chapter 23

THE SUN WAS BRIGHT enough out the window when Papa called them to get up for Jordan to figure they'd missed the bus. Papa must have overslept. Today they would not go to school. Papa never bothered to drive them there late.

Jordan jumped out of bed and quickly slipped into her dress.

"Get up, you lazy sleeper!" she called to Brother, shaking him by the shoulders. Brother grumbled and pulled himself to sit up in his bed. "Here." Jordan handed him his glasses and sat on the floor to pull on her shoes.

"I'll go get our breakfast. No school today. Papa's calling." Brother got to his feet at that and Jordan went to get the cereal.

Papa sat eating eggs and sausage. "Good day for fishing today," he said, grinning. Papa was in a good mood. That was good.

Last night he was angry at Jordan for not washing the dishes. There had been no more detergent. And that was

Jordan's fault for using too much before. There should have been enough left. If she hadn't wasted it.

But now the sun was high and Papa seemed to have forgotten all about last night.

Jordan poured out the cereal, set the milk out, and ran off to hurry Brother along. They'd be getting a late start as it was. She found him coming through the hall to the kitchen.

"Good," she whispered, "Papa's taking us fishing today. Hurry, we gotta eat quick."

The little white cat meowed loudly from the back screen. It had found them. Followed the rabbit paths from the marsh through the scrub to the backyard.

Papa won't like it, Jordan thought. "Go away," she said, raising her spoon to scare it off.

"You haven't been giving that cat anything to eat?" Papa looked at the children.

Brother shook his head no.

"No, Papa," Jordan said.

"That's a feral cat," Papa said.

"What's that, Papa?" Brother asked.

"Wild cat," Papa said. "Stray."

"I'll go run her off," Jordan said, going to the door and opening it. The cat came in.

It walked over and rubbed its head against the leg of a chair. Papa kicked gently at it, pushed it down and held it, his foot on top of its neck. And he laughed. The cat struggled and slipped out, hissing. Jordan grabbed it. "I'll put her out, Papa," she said, backing onto the screen porch. The little cat felt warm and soft in her arms. And she went to the backyard and put it down.

"You're a *sweet* little cat," she whispered. It moved and stopped, looking back.

"Go away," she said. "You mustn't come here." It scampered off into the brush toward the marsh, and she breathed deeply.

She did give it something the other day ... Saturday ... the piece of hot dog they saved on the day they went to the ocean. She did, and she must never, never do that.

Jordan ran back to the house and slipped into her chair at the table.

"She's gone now," Jordan said.

"She better be," Papa said. "If she comes back here, she just might find a bullet in her head." Jordan looked up, startled. She opened her mouth but closed it. She must not argue back. He was just talking anyway. He wouldn't do that. She glanced at Brother and shoveled down her cereal, soggy now. Papa was ready to go.

Chapter 24

A MILE DOWN THE road toward town, past the river, and almost to the shrimp boat docks, a small bridge crossed one of the creeks embedded in the miles of marshes that spread out on both sides of the road to town. To one side, a dock and an old tackle shop, to the other, a short sandy road leading down to the water. Papa pulled off on the road and stopped the car.

Jordan and Brother waited in the musty smell of the back seat. The breeze off the marsh drifted in the open windows, but the air in the car was thick with growing heat. Jordan and Brother waited until Papa got out.

"Carson, get on 'round here," Papa called, and Brother went to the trunk to help Papa with the nets and lines and bait. Jordan went to the muddy sand at the edge of the creek and smiled at an old man who stood fishing. He touched his cap and spoke to her, then turned back to his line. Jordan surveyed the two other fishers. She liked talking to them. But Papa had told her to keep her mouth shut and not bother people. So Jordan just smiled, and sat by the water's edge and picked among the small chipped shells and stones, searching for one that was not broken. She would try to keep her mouth shut. She would sit and be good. She would not bother anyone.

She thought of the little white cat. It was her fault it came this morning. If it came back, it was her fault.

It must not come back.

The sun began to burn at her arms. It would be a hot day. Her arms would get red. Her nose would peel. She would go back to school and take a note about being out sick and her nose would peel and her arms and face would be red from the sun.

She went to the car and got the bag of cheese chips out of the back seat. She ate standing by the open car door. The breeze lifted her limp hair a bit, cooling her neck. She noticed another car coming off the road. The man sat in his car and she looked at him through his open window. He had a high forehead and black hair. His cheekbones were high, also, and prominent. The straight nose, deep set eyes, wide chin, thick neck. She had seen him before.

In time, Brother came to Jordan and they sat together on the back of the car to talk so they would not disturb the fishermen. Then the man got out of the car and went to Papa by the water.

Jordan and Brother took off their socks and shoes. They ate the rest of the cheese chips. They played a game with the cars going by up on the road. Colors. Picking a color and seeing who had the most cars of their color go by.

And Jordan noticed the familiar man and Papa again. Something about the way they talked, like it was a secret, she did not like. And a laugh. She did not like the laugh. And then the man left.

"Do you know that man?" Jordan asked Brother.

Brother squinted at the man as he got in his car. His sleeveless black T-shirt looked dusty and faded and his eyes were covered now with sunglasses.

"A man from the house?" Brother questioned. "A friend of Papa?"

The man's car turned, raising clouds of dust, and he left, heading in the direction of town.

"Maybe," Jordan said. "I think so." And she stared after the car long after it was gone.

"Why do you think we came so late today?" Brother asked. "Here to fish. Why do you think?" The sun blazed out of the sky, burning at their skin. It was lunchtime.

"Maybe it's a better time to catch fish," Jordan said. "Or maybe that man. Maybe Papa knew that man was coming."

She looked down the road again. What was it about that man? Why did he sit in his car and wait till she and Brother had both left Papa before he went over there? Why should that man care about that?

Chapter 25

A SHRIMP BOAT INCHED through a winding channel in the marsh on its way back from the sea. Jordan and Brother sat on the trunk of the car and looked across the road trying to make out the trawler's name. It moved toward the deep docks on the big creek where some of the boats came in.

Mama took them one time, when Jordan was just six, to those deep docks. It was when Mama's uncle, Grandpa's brother, had come to visit.

His name was Uncle Bob and he was a retired man with grown kids and glasses thick as Brother's, and who always dressed in white starched shirts and gray pants and who was a man of few words.

"She talks enough for both of us," he joked about his wife, Viv, and it was true. Aunt Viv had lots to say, and Mama liked her.

"Remember Uncle Bob and Aunt Viv?" Jordan said. Brother shook his head no. Jordan breathed in the strong, salty smells of the wetlands.

"Reckon they know about Mama?" Jordan said. She

squinted at the boat. Uncle Bob and Aunt Viv would want to know what was going on.

Did Papa tell them about Mama, and that's why they never came down anymore? Wouldn't they want to see her and Brother? Did Papa tell them not to come?

Something had happened to keep them away.

The shrimp boat had stopped now to unload its catch over at the docks where they went that day years ago.

Perhaps Uncle Bob could see the way Papa never did like Mama's people. Maybe that's why they didn't visit at the house that day. And Papa had not come to the docks with them.

Those docks were made of the thickest, strongest planks and posts Jordan had ever seen. The boats were right up close where they could see in the cabins even, and they'd talked to some of the shrimpers, and Mama's Uncle Bob had bags of lemon drops for Jordan and Brother and for Mama, too.

Chapter 26

THAT NIGHT THEY had fish. Papa had taken them home in the afternoon and told them to clean the fish. Told them he was going to get some paint for a job he was doing for someone. Left them to open a can of pork and beans and make hot dogs and eat their midafternoon lunch on the back steps with their plates balanced on their knees because he was not there to say no.

"This is like a cookout," Jordan told Brother. A little brown bird lit on the edge of the brambles toward the marsh and then flitted away. Jordan and Brother watched him as they ate their hot dogs.

"I'm glad we stayed out of school," Brother replied. "I'm glad we had this cookout."

Jordan and Brother worked on cleaning the fish after that, in an old sink in the yard, and put them in the refrigerator to wait for suppertime. Papa came home at sundown. He had flour and cornmeal and onions and they watched him mix the batter and fry the fish and hush puppies.

The white cat appeared at the back screen again, meowing loudly, begging for the fish.

"You better be glad my hands are full," Papa said, shaking the large fork at the cat.

Jordan hurried to the door. "I'll make her go," she said, bending down to catch the cat as she opened the screen. She took her, curled in her arms, out to the front road and told her to go somewhere else. She *had* to go somewhere else. "Scat!" she yelled and the cat hesitated and then tripped off toward the lights of another house. Jordan watched her go, silvery in the light of the moon, with a little pang in her heart. "Don't come back," she whispered.

They ate the fish dinner in the yellow light of the kitchen with the sweet summerlike air floating in the open windows, drenched with the scent of honeysuckle and the singing of crickets outside. Jordan and Brother laughed and patted their full bellies and said they were stuffed. Then Papa laughed at them when they both wanted the last hush puppy. "Your old man did pretty good today, didn't he?" Papa said, and Jordan and Brother grinned and shook their heads yes.

Chapter 27

Papa went out that night. Jordan saw him tuck something under his charcoal sweatshirt before he left. She saw him as she turned and glanced in his room while handing a dish to Brother to dry, right before Papa came out and called a man named Jim, and said he was leaving now. Something about it all seemed wrong to Jordan.

She glanced at Brother. He hadn't noticed anything. What if she imagined it?

Like Mama imagined things.

Jordan and Brother sat together on the cinder block steps out the front door when they finished the dishes. The night air had cooled.

They heard a car coming and watched it go by down the dark road, its lights splashing over the asphalt as it passed.

"Where does Papa go at night?" Brother asked.

"To see his friends," Jordan said, her eyes on the lights in the house across the road. No one had been there for some time. Tonight the lights were on again. Someone had come for the weekend.

"Papa was happy today," Brother said. "Why do you think he was so happy?"

"Perhaps he got the money," Jordan said. "Perhaps he got a job."

"Summer's coming," Brother said. "Renters. There'll be work. Papa'll have lots of work, don't you think?"

"Yeah," Jordan said, "I think that's it." She watched people moving inside the house across the street. People with money to rent houses for the weekend. People who came with bright-colored lawn chairs and chests full of ice that they put on the decks.

A rat scurried across the drive into the weeds. Jordan and Brother watched in silence. A shadow, a movement became the white cat. It was after the rat. "I told you to go!" Jordan stood and started down the steps. She picked up a stick and threw it, carefully, so it wouldn't go far. So it wouldn't hit the cat.

And then the cat was gone.

Chapter 28

JORDAN WOKE UP ON the sofa, the house dark, the television still going, and someone knocking at the door. She looked around, confused. Was Papa home? No, he would have sent her to bed if he had found her here. Brother sat up in his chair, too, wiping his eyes and looking at the door. Jordan glanced back at him and put her finger to her mouth and they sat. The knocking came again. Papa had told them, "Do not let anyone know you are here alone."

So they sat and waited. A voice called out. A young man's voice.

"Ronny!" he called. Brother crawled over and turned the TV off.

"Ronny," the voice called again.

Then a woman's voice. "Maybe the kids are there. . . . Jordan . . . I think the girl's named Jordan."

"Jordan? Open up in there!" the man called. And then silence. Jordan remained on the sofa, and Brother sitting on the floor by the television, watching first the door, then each other.

"Open up," the man called. More talking between the man and the woman. Some cursing.

"You tell your daddy he's paying me. I'll be back 'round here later this evenin'." Then the solid metal thud of a truck door closing. Two doors. And lights through the windows, and the sound of the pickup leaving in the driveway.

Later that night, Jordan woke in her bed and heard the crunch of a car through the old gravel drive, the hum of a motor. Then silence. Some minutes went by before the slam of the car door and Papa coming in.

A little later the same voice from earlier, only in the house now. And Papa's voice, real friendly. "Told you I'd have it tonight," Papa said. And the other voice was friendly now, too.

Chapter 29

OWN THE ROAD from Jordan's house was the post office where Papa would pick up his mail since there was no delivery to houses on the island. Jordan and Brother had gone with him and stood outside waiting.

A van was parked by the walk. ANIMAL CONTROL it said. Jordan went over to the woman who got out. "Have you got lost animals in there?" she asked.

"One dog," the officer said, "but it might be a stray. There's no collar." She tilted her head. "Have you lost a dog?"

"No." Jordan smiled.

Brother stood behind Jordan, his uncombed hair sticking up on top. He stood on tiptoe trying to see in the window of the van.

"Can we see it?" Jordan asked. Brother looked back at the woman.

"Well, maybe it would be better to get your mama to take you to the shelter to look at the animals. You can adopt them, you know."

Jordan nodded at the lady. "Do you ever see feral cats?"

"Feral cats! Yes, there are a few on the island."

"Feral cats are nice," Jordan said.

"They are. But feral cats are really wild, you know. I've heard of people who've tamed them . . . especially the kittens, but feral cats are terrified of people. Sometimes people think abandoned cats are ferals."

Jordan thought a moment. The white cat wasn't feral, it was abandoned. Whichever, Papa didn't like it. And neither did whoever abandoned it.

"Some people don't like stray cats," Jordan said.

"Some people do complain about stray cats making a real mess looking in garbage cans for food. And then there's the rabies threat."

Jordan glanced at the van. That dog in there had no collar.

"But cats don't need collars, do they?" Jordan asked.

"A collar would be very helpful, but they need a special safety collar, so they won't get hurt. And they need their tags."

"For their names," Jordan said.

"Yes, but mostly they need the owner's name, address, or phone, so we can find them. And of course cats needs their rabies tag up to date."

Jordan watched a man with a long beard and ponytail park his bike on the grass, and she thought about what the officer had said. She looked back up at the woman.

"Do you have cat safety collars that you can give to people?" Jordan asked.

The woman smiled at Jordan. "Do you have a cat?" she asked.

"What if it don't have a collar and a tag?" Brother asked.

"Well, if someone called to complain about a cat like that, a cat that wasn't in its yard, and was causing trouble, we'd take it and try to find its owner, and if we couldn't we'd try to find it a good home."

Jordan's face was suddenly solemn. A squawking bird sound came from the bushy wooded lots across the street.

"Papa says you kill them if you can't," Jordan said.

"No. Some places do, but we have a wonderful place that keeps the cats until they find a home."

Jordan glanced at Brother. Who should she believe? This lady? Or her own papa?

"If someone calls you about a white cat with green eyes, she's already got a home. We just don't have her a collar for her tag yet, but you don't need to pick her up . . . if you see one like that," Jordan said. She gazed confidently at the officer.

"That girl bothering you?" Jordan flinched at Papa's voice behind her.

"Oh, no!" The officer laughed. "Your daughter's just asking some questions."

"Don't surprise me none," Papa said. "Just goes up

and talks to strangers, don't matter none to her. She'll turn out just like her mama."

Suddenly Jordan was aware of heat rising from the little parking lot. Cars coming and going. And there was shade next door over by the back of the little church with the stained glass. When Jordan was about six, they would walk down to that church, Mama and herself and Brother, and they would look at the statue in the front and at the windows.

It was the statue that talked to Mama and it was the windows with the pictures that talked to Mama and they would not talk to Jordan though she tried very hard to hear them.

"I was just going to tell her about the rabies clinic here every year." The officer's words broke into her thoughts. "There'll be one in less than a month. Why don't you bring in your cat then?"

Papa laughed. "Shoot, we ain't got no cat."

"Oh. I just . . . I guess I misunderstood. I thought maybe she had a pet cat."

"Hell, no," Papa said. "Now you two leave the lady be. Can't you see she's got a job to do?"

Jordan stared at the palmettos across the road. An old man with dark skin and frizzled white hair stood cutting some fronds off, putting them in the trunk of his car.

"Oh, they were no bother," the officer was saying.

"Even so. It ain't like she ain't been told to keep her mouth shut enough times."

Papa started off down the road to home, Brother following, glancing back at Jordan.

Jordan did not look up at the officer. Her face burned with shame from being caught in a lie. She ran to catch up with Brother and Papa, listening again to the cry of the squawking bird in the woods.

Chapter 30

THE NEXT DAY AT school Jordan smelled fried fish cooking in the lunchroom and she knew the white cat would love that fish. What the animal control lady said about garbage cans and strays causing a mess, the white cat wouldn't have to do that, Jordan thought, if she could give it some of that fish. Then it wouldn't be out turning over cans and getting caught by the lady in the van.

She had to feed the cat.

All morning long when Jordan smelled the fish frying she thought about it, and at lunch, Jordan put the fish from her plate on her napkin and when one of the girls with shiny clean hair and pretty new clothes said she was going to tell the teacher what Jordan had done with her food, Jordan explained, "I don't like fish and I don't like it on my plate."

"You always like everything," said the girl.

"Not fish," Jordan said, and when the girl looked away Jordan slipped it down into her lap where a folded pocket made of notebook paper waited, a pocket she had prepared back in the room covered with some class work, folded over once, as a disguise.

Jordan almost dropped her tray, carrying it with the white cat's fish, all wrapped up, balanced under the tray, and the paper was beginning to look greasy, but Jordan held it casually by her side in the line, and luckily no one seemed to be paying any more attention to her than usual that day. Jordan felt warm and happy inside when she thought of showing Brother what she had for the cat and them going to find it somewhere down the road if Papa wasn't around.

Later that afternoon Jordan sat in the guidance counselor's office. Someone had told. And she had had to take the fish back to the lunchroom and throw it away.

The guidance counselor wanted to know why she took the fish. Was she hungry at home?

Jordan said she just didn't like it and had taken it off her plate and then forgot to throw it away when she put up her tray, but that she was going to throw it away when it was time to get on the bus.

The guidance counselor said she wanted Jordan to feel free to tell her if she ever needed anything.

Jordan did not want the counselor getting any ideas about sending the social worker to her house. Papa would be really mad if they came about this fish.

"We don't need anything," Jordan said quickly, "and we can do practically anything and get away with it now.

He doesn't even beat us . . . Papa, I mean, doesn't. Or anything else either . . . not even get mad."

The counselor listened to all Jordan had to say. "Are you sure there's nothing bothering you? You look kind of sad," she said.

Well, yes. Jordan was sad that they made her throw away the white cat's dinner. After all it was her fish, off her plate. They had no right to make her throw it away, and she was mad at them all, and she would show them. She would get some food for the cat . . . somehow . . . they could not stop her.

Chapter 31

WHEN THE COUNSELOR asked Jordan if she'd like to stay awhile and look at the aquarium, Jordan said "No," although she really would have kind of liked to have stayed. But Jordan went back to class. She did not look at any of them.

After school, she would make a new plan to feed the cat. She would find something it could eat so it wouldn't get caught, wouldn't go to a shelter, because they killed animals sometimes at shelters, Papa said.

When school was over, Jordan went by the cafeteria on her way out thinking maybe she could ask the ladies in there if they had any leftovers that a starving cat would like, because she knew one.

The tables stood folded and clean and rolled to the corners of the spotless floor and the door of the kitchen was open, but everything was all put away, and very quiet, and the ladies seemed to have already gone home.

Jordan saw the bus line out by the breezeway already

moving. She ran and climbed up the steep school bus steps.

Brother didn't know about the trouble with the fish at lunch, but Jordan told him.

"Do you think we could get something to feed the cat from home, Jordie?" Brother wanted to know.

Jordan said, "We could take sandwich meat. Papa wouldn't notice if we took a piece."

Brother liked the idea. "I bet we can find that cat at the dock."

"That's too close to the house. We don't want her coming around for food at the house. You know what Papa said. We'll go to that dirt road in the woods at the end of the street and look."

"But Papa don't allow us down there."

"We'll wait till Papa leaves. We'll take water and a water bowl, too. Papa won't miss it. He doesn't eat cereal."

"Two bowls," Brother said. "One for the food."

Jordan and Brother sat back thinking about the plan and hoping Papa would go off somewhere soon, maybe even today, so they could try it out.

The road narrowed to two lanes and the bus rolled through the acres and acres of marshes signaling they would soon be home.

And off in the distance were thick groups of trees that Jordan thought must be little wild islands where only animals lived. She turned to watch. Water birds rose from the marshes. Beautiful, brilliantly white birds with startling black legs, rising over the green grasses and soaring against the deep blue clouds building in the sky.

Chapter 32

THE CAT DID NOT get fed that day after school. Papa did not leave, and, besides, the next morning Jordan looked and there was no sandwich meat left anyway. She hoped Papa would get some today.

"We're going with Papa," Jordan explained. "We're going to collect bricks. Hurry!" Brother carried his toast with him and followed Jordan. They climbed in the back seat of the old car and waited. The air was still and stuffy. They struggled with the windows, rolling them down. It was hard because they stuck. The morning was early yet, but the day promised to be hot.

"Are we going the same place?" Brother asked, for they had been with Papa before to collect salvage materials.

"No. Somewhere new," Jordan said.

Brother crawled up on his knees and looked out the back of the car. "Will the bus stop and blow its horn this morning?" he asked.

"No. If we aren't at the road, I think it'll go on by."

Brother turned back around and slipped down on

the torn upholstery of the seat. He picked at it, ripping the tear and exposing white lining.

Last night Brother had asked Papa when Mama would be coming to see them again. "Don't worry 'bout your mama. She ain't worrying about you," Papa had said. Brother had started picking at the sofa then, until Papa told him to stop.

Now he picked out some lining from the car seat and rolled it between his palms.

"Better not," Jordan said, frowning. She watched him. The little house sat silent in the early light out her window, dew dripping slowly off the roof by the door.

"What Papa said about Mama last night. It's not true," she said.

Brother threw her a glance.

"Mama's in the state hospital."

"She's sick?" Brother cried. "How can she be sick so long, Jordie?"

"It's not like if you're sick and gonna die. She's lost her mind. I heard it at school. . . . I heard where she is."

Brother stared at her, his mouth slightly open.

"You know what that means?"

Brother shrugged.

"It means . . . sometimes she gets real mixed up . . . too mixed up . . . like she thinks things are happening that aren't really there."

They looked at each other. The sun trickled through the back window lighting little stray pieces of their hair.

"Will she ever come back?" Brother asked.

Jordan looked at the house . . . at the little chimney from the buck stove . . . at a shadow it cast on the old tin roof. The green paint on the old tin roof. "They didn't say," she said.

Brother stuffed the lining back in the seat. They heard children's voices from a few blocks toward the ocean, waiting for the bus, and a whistlelike call from a bird.

They sat and waited, thinking of Mama and wondering.

Chapter 33

PAPA DROVE WAY INTO the country and pulled off down a long drive leading to a deserted yard. Remains of an old house baked in the sun. There were piles of brick. Papa opened the trunk and backed it as close as he could. He gave the children gloves too big for their hands and told them to fill as much as they could into the back seat while he filled the trunk. He put gloves on his hands and stared down the road that led to the old house, then took Jordan by the arm and led her into the drive in front of the car.

"Watch that road. Let me know if anyone turns down this drive," he said.

Jordan watched, but none of the cars turned off. Papa switched Brother to the watch after he grew tired. Then Jordan worked. It was slow. The bricks were heavy.

She was troubled by the watching. Who were they watching for? It was better not to ask. If Papa wanted her to know he would tell her. She kept glancing to the road each time she dumped a brick in the car. But no one came.

The morning passed slowly. Papa gave them cans of soda to drink and a bag of crackers. Before noon they were finished. Papa said they might come for another load some other time. Now he would take them home and go sell the brick.

Chapter 34

JORDAN AND BROTHER compared blisters on their hands, their feet curled under them behind the bricks on the floor, the fresh air whipping in the windows and blowing their hair. At last the familiar smell of salt air as they rode over the bridges toward home. Papa let them out. They could go to the store and buy something to eat if they needed, he said, and he left them with their key to the house and five dollars. They looked in the kitchen. They were too tired to walk to the store, so they decided they would just have the rest of the bread with butter and jelly and drink the rest of the grape soda.

They would save the five dollars. They would tell Papa they got something from the machines at the convenience store and they would save the five dollars for something special some day.

"We could even get something for the white cat," Jordan said.

"A collar!" Brother said.

"Yeah! Then no one would take her!" Jordan said. "I think she would like a collar."

She put the bread on plates and started spreading butter on the slices.

She handed the knife to Brother. He liked to spread his own bread.

After lunch Jordan and Brother took the five dollars and walked to a little store, weathered and grayed by salt air, and they looked for a collar for the white cat. A safety collar. They saw surfboards and floats blown up and shaped like porpoises and little cedar boxes that said AT-LANTIC OCEAN and pretty picture postcards of the beach and lots of other things but no collars for cats.

"Up the road toward town," the man said. "There's a pet store. That's where you need to go." But Jordan and Brother could not think of a way to get there.

Jordan handed the five dollars to Brother and he stuffed it in his pocket. They would save it for the cat's collar, they would put it away and only use it for that, nothing else. It was the cat's money now.

They went home and were still tired and went to sleep in front of the television. When they woke, it was late. About six. Papa was still gone. They were hungry and Papa should be back now.

Jordan turned off the television. The house had a still gray light.

"Who do you think we were watching for today?" Brother asked, still sitting in Papa's chair.

Jordan looked at him from the window where she had been watching for Papa. She gazed back out to the road. The window was open and the summerlike air stirred gently. A chill ran over her.

"Who do you think?" Brother asked again.

Jordan sighed and went to the sofa. "Perhaps it was someone who owned the place," Jordan said.

"Do you think we were stealing today, Jordie?" Brother asked.

He knew. They were probably stealing. But she didn't want to say it. They looked at each other in the cool vague light. A car hummed by outside. And another. And a dog barked far off.

"Do you think Papa will come back soon?" Brother asked finally.

Jordan felt the hunger growing in her belly. There wasn't anything but some stale crackers and some old pickles. Some vegetable cans. Nothing any good for them to make for supper.

She felt unsettled. Didn't Papa know they were waiting for supper? Where was he?

"Surely he will be back soon," Jordan said.

Chapter 35

PAPA ENTERED THE room without looking at the children. "Food's in the car." He moved his head in the direction of the front door and Brother went out, coming back with two large grocery bags. Jordan put them away. Papa sat in the living room now. Jordan went to the door. Her stomach gnawed at her. She could almost smell the food he brought cooking.

"Supper, Papa?" she asked.

He turned his head and looked at her. His eyes narrowed slightly, his mouth set in a thin line, almost a frown.

Jordan backed away slightly. "You want me to fix supper, Papa?" she asked.

The mouth curled up slightly. "You hungry, girl?"

"I just thought . . . it was time," Jordan said. The silence of the room smothered her. There was nothing outside. No cars going by. No birds. Just silence. And Papa. And she shouldn't have asked about supper.

Papa shook his head up and down ever so slightly as

he continued to gaze at Jordan. "Why don't ya just say you're hungry?" he asked finally.

Jordan stared, her eyes wide and dark in the dim light, her heart beating harder in her chest. She said nothing.

"Go ahead, say it," Papa said.

"I'm hungry," Jordan mumbled.

Papa glared at her. The look of resentment, of blame, growing on his face.

What had she done now? She felt the fear growing inside. She felt the rage swelling in her heart. Brother came and stood behind her.

"Two little snivilin' . . . ," Papa muttered. "Get out here," he yelled suddenly. "Both of you. Get out here where I can see you."

Jordan and Brother went in the room. Moved into the room slowly . . . not looking or seeing . . . just feeling . . . and knowing.

"Just so you two don't go running off at the mouth, you keep in mind I have to pay for this place. . . . Anybody asks you something, anybody at that school of yours, you didn't go anywhere with me today. Understand?" He stopped and looked at them. "You know what's good for you, you'll do like I say."

The veins on Papa's neck bulged as he spoke. Jordan watched the veins on his neck. Outside some voices way down the street, children on bikes. A car. Birds. But inside the house, silence.

"You got it?" Papa shouted.

Jordan and Brother flinched. "Yes, sir," Jordan said.

"Yes, sir," Brother echoed.

"Go on an get y' supper," Papa growled, slumping back in his chair.

"You want some?" Jordan asked. "You want me to fix you some?"

The blare of the television surprised her as Papa pointed the remote at the set and laughed as she jumped. He eyed her for a moment. "Nah, I don't need any."

He had already had something to eat, before he came home. He had had something already, Jordan thought, while they sat at home hungry.

Well, the white cat was out there hungry, too. Jordan was going to feed her and she would not wait until Papa left. That might be too late. It had already been three days since the cat came begging at the screen door. She wanted to take it some food now. She wanted to take it that food Papa brought home. And she would. She would go down the road where she had seen it and take it some of that food when they finished eating . . . when Papa seemed settled in front of the television.

Jordan and Brother crept into the kitchen. They got out the orange soda and made toasted cheese sandwiches. They ate in silence, eyeing the door to the kitchen.

They ate quickly, so they could leave, go outside, get out of his way. So they would not be there when he got out of that chair.

Jordan thought of the five dollars they had saved and a new collar for the white cat ... a safety collar ... blue ... or a green one, to match the white cat's green eyes.

And Jordan wondered, did they make green collars for cats?

Chapter 36

BROTHER SAT BESIDE Jordan on the back steps, nervous, knowing what she had told him while the toasted cheese sandwiches had cooked in the oven, while she filled a small plastic grocery bag with an old soda bottle full of tap water, a slice of sandwich meat, and two green plastic cereal bowls.

Now the bag was under the screen porch and Jordan sat with her chin in her hand and the air hung heavy in the lateness of the day. She listened for the sounds, the familiar sounds from the house, from the television, to settle in.

"We aren't allowed." Brother's eyes were scared.

"But the white cat *must* be hungry," Jordan whispered.

Brother watched her. She had never been so determined. It frightened him. Nevertheless he followed her through the woods by the side of their house and past a big house with a wide yard to where the asphalt stopped and the dirt road began.

Old oyster shells lay crushed in the sand and ferns

grew in clusters by the side of the road. A big log lay in a clearing where they could see to the river. They listened to the wind in the oaks above. A swarm of tiny, translucent insects swirled in the shadows.

"Does someone live down here, Jordie?" Brother asked.

"There's a car," Jordan said. "Way down there. We won't go that far."

Brother peered down the road. Everything was still. "Do you think we should call it for supper?" he asked. "I think we should call."

Jordan called softly. "Here kitty kitty. Here kitty. We've got some food for you." Her eyes darted between the stillness of the trees and bushes.

"*Here* kitty kitty," Jordan called again and they listened and it was quiet and woodsy with sweet leafy smells and they sat there together on a big log, waiting. Hoping.

And then it was time to go.

The white cat did not come that day.

"Can we leave the food here behind the log?" Brother asked.

Jordan's face lit up. "Yes! And we'll come see if it's gone." She scrambled over the log and set the bowls down in little scooped-out places she dug. She filled the water bowl.

"It looks like a little pond, doesn't it?" she said.

Brother started tearing up the meat into little pieces. "Cats like little pieces," he said, dropping it into the other bowl.

They walked back to the pavement in the fading light. They looked toward their house, and it seemed a very long way to go if someone might suddenly come out from behind those trees, and stand in that road, and find out you had disobeyed and left the property.

They ran. Jordan tripped and skinned her knee. Brother stopped at the woods looking back and forth at the road one way and the other.

"Jordie!" he yelled. "Come on!"

Jordan got up. She glanced at her knee. It wasn't bad, and she ran to catch up. They went through the woods and around to the back steps where they sat catching their breath and thinking of a sandy road in a silent little woods with birds and chirping insects and a little pond and some fresh food just waiting there as night came on.

"Why didn't you come when I called?" Papa stood behind them on the back porch.

Jordan tried to explain she didn't hear. She didn't say why she didn't hear. She didn't say where she had been. She hoped he would think they were back by the river.

She got a beating with the belt. Not for not coming when he called, or for where they had been. Papa didn't realize where they had been. But for talking back. Jordan only meant to be explaining, but Papa thought it was the wrong tone. And Brother got a beating, too. For whining. It was the wrong tone. It was important to not use the wrong tone with Papa.

Chapter 37

THE NEXT DAY JORDAN and Brother went to school with the blisters on their hands from the bricks. They would say they got them on the monkey bars anyway, if anyone asked. Lots of kids got blisters on the monkey bars. No one noticed.

Papa was gone when they got home from school. Jordan sat on the back steps. There was the tin sound of a radio playing some ways off in the distance. The rental house maybe . . . or somewhere farther.

In a while Brother came and stood before her. "My blisters hurt," he said, holding out his hands. The blisters were open.

Jordan pushed her hair away from her face. The radio kept on, faint but clear. An old rock and roll song. The kind Mama liked.

"You shouldn't have done that," Jordan said. "I told you not to pop them."

"I didn't," Brother said.

Jordan found some peroxide in the bathroom for Brother, but he wanted Band-Aids. There were none in the bathroom so she climbed on a chair to look high in the kitchen cabinet. An old stack of papers caught her eye, a letter on the stack, and she climbed down with it.

"What is it?" Brother asked.

"It's from Mama's Uncle Bob. It's old," Jordan said. "I told you about Uncle Bob. Remember?"

Brother scrunched his face. "Sort of," he said.

Jordan pointed to the corner of the letter. "That's where Uncle Bob lives," she said. "That's his address." And Jordan knew then someone to send a card to. She knew just the card she would send to Uncle Bob and Aunt Viv. One with a picture of a beautiful black Labrador retriever.

She got it from her room and held it out for Brother to see. "They'll like this, don't you think?" Jordan said.

Brother nodded, grinning.

Jordan and Brother went to the kitchen table with the card, and Jordan started writing.

Dear Uncle Bob and Aunt Viv,

Remember when you came and took us to see the shrimp boats? That was so much fun.

Brother is eight now and I am eleven.

I don't know if you know it but Mama got put in the state hospital.

Papa went on a job yesterday and we went to help him and did not have to go to school.

love,

Jordan

Jordan pushed the card over to Brother. "Here, you can sign it, too. Right there." She pointed under her name.

Brother took the pencil and wrote "and Carson" under Jordan's name. He held out the card to admire the picture of the dog. "They'll be surprised, won't they, to get this picture," he said.

"They'll be real surprised," Jordan agreed. She copied the address from the old letter onto the card. The sound of a car made Jordan look up. "We'll have to wait till Papa sends us to get the mail." Brother nodded. Jordan handed him the card. "Papa doesn't like Uncle Bob, so don't tell," she said, and Brother ran off to put the card away.

Chapter 38

S ATURDAY MORNING, Papa told Jordan to go get his mail from the post office.

"We can go check on the white cat's bowls," Jordan whispered to Brother, her face beaming. She stood in the kitchen stuffing a bag with food in her pocket. "Then we'll go get Papa's mail, and mail our card. And if Papa calls, he'll just think we're still at the post office."

The bowls were still behind the log and, sure enough, something had been there and eaten the food. Though Jordan and Brother knew it could have been raccoons or other animals, they also knew the white cat had been seen there on that very road, and they couldn't help thinking it was the white cat who found and ate the food.

They looked and called and left more food and water and ran to the post office with the card and some change for a stamp and then ran home. They handed Papa his mail and his mailbox key, and they went and sat on the old dock in the warm noonday sun. The river shone blue and sparkling way out past the grasses. They listened to the sound of a redbird nearby and thought about the surprise Uncle Bob and Aunt Viv would be getting in their mailbox and about the surprise they left in the woods for the white cat.

Chapter 39

THE NEXT NIGHT that Papa decided to go out, Jordan and Brother went, too. Papa told them to get in the back seat and said he was taking them out for hamburgers.

So they left the salt air and the great sweeping marshes and drove on down toward town where the bright colored lights of the burger chains lit up the roadside. Papa ordered them a take-out, a bag of cheeseburgers and fries wrapped in thin, brightly colored paper that sat in a cardboard tray beside cups of soda with plastic tops. Jordan breathed in the smells from the back seat where she waited, trying to be patient. And she would save a piece of hamburger for the white cat, too. Brother sat up and leaned over the front seat eyeing the treats.

"Sit back," Papa said. "Sit back and hold your horses." So Brother sat back and Jordan and Brother held their horses as Papa drove to another place along the road. BAR AND GRILL, it said in neon lights.

Papa said, "You two go ahead and eat. Then wait

here. I'll be back after a while." He gave them the tray with the cups and the bag and left them in the darkening day sitting in the car with the windows down, waiting in the sandy parking lot. The sky, just a hint of purple light left in the west, backdropped the silhouette of the shabby roadhouse.

Jordan divided the treats from the bag, Brother poked the straws through the little holes in the plastic lids, and they felt like very lucky children eating their meals as the soft summer air stirred in and out of the open windows. Cars came and went from the bar and grill. People got out and walked through the lot, paying no mind to the two children in the back seat of the dusty old car.

Jordan and Brother leaned back into the upholstery sucking soda through the straws, a full, satisfied feeling in their middles.

From time to time, they got up on their knees and looked out the back window at the cars hurrying by on the highway. Jordan sat back down and pulled the plastic cup cover off. The little squares of ice were a treat, too. She sucked them one at a time. The sky changed to a heavy black, then rumbled in the distance toward the city. The air became cooler and all the little ice squares were gone.

Jordan rested her chin on her folded arms in the window. Her face felt cool and the breeze played with her hair.

A figure appeared coming out of the dark cavelike

door of the low-slung tavern, and another figure, and they got in a car and rode away.

"That looked like Papa," Brother said.

Jordan looked toward the sky over the city. Sheet lightning flickered. "It was Papa," she said. The light came again in the sky.

"Where's he going?" Brother asked, and Jordan was quiet.

Brother said, "Maybe he thought of a better place to go."

Jordan breathed in the cool air. She was fairly sure that Papa did not think they had seen him leave. . . . Why would Papa think they wouldn't see? Why did Papa think they didn't know things?

Brother bit on his straw. Jordan watched the sky. The lightning came less and less until it was no more. Her lids grew heavy. The white cat's hamburger would be spoiled. She would have to throw it out.

She looked back at Brother. He was sleeping, leaned back in the corner on his side. Jordan wondered when Papa would come back. She leaned into her corner and closed her eyes, too. The sounds of the traffic and the people who came and went to the bar faded, then came louder, then became part of her dream.

Chapter 40

J ORDAN WOKE TO THE CAR door, and Papa was starting the engine, racing the motor a little before pulling out to the road. Jordan and Brother sat up, putting their arms on the back of the front seat.

"That supper was *sooo* good," Jordan said.

"*Sooo, sooo* good," Brother said.

"I thought you two would like that," Papa said. He laughed.

Sometimes Papa was nice, Jordan thought. Like tonight, getting them the take-out.

Two shining eyes crossed the road in front of them as they neared the marshes. "Look at that possum," Papa said, speeding up the car.

"Papa! You'll hit it," Jordan cried.

Papa laughed. "Not that one, but I've gotten some of 'em comin' 'long here nights."

"You mean . . . ?" Jordan stopped. Papa tried to hit them? How could he? Why? Why would someone want to do that? Jordan felt sick. And she was just thinking about the way that Papa was nice. Papa was not nice.

Her fingers grasped the back of the seat and she watched, hoping no more shining pairs of eyes would come across the road. Don't any more come, she thought. And no more came. They crossed the bridge and turned down the road to the house.

"It's early but you kids need to get on to bed," Papa said, "no television," and Jordan remembered thinking of that later. She remembered thinking it was funny Papa would say it was early. It wasn't early at all.

Chapter 41

LATE THE NEXT DAY the sky was a soft deep blue and the moon already hung low through the trees toward the east when Brother came running. Jordan was on the back porch rocking.

"Come see!" Brother said, appearing outside the screen.

Jordan looked up, surprised.

"It's down there, Jordie! I saw it! The white cat is down there now!"

Jordan jumped up. "Hurry, Jordie. It'll leave," he said, and they ran to the edge of the yard and looked down the road and there it was, just at the woods, near where they had left the food.

"I'm going to take it something!" Jordan said, her face flushed.

Brother grabbed her arm as she turned, but she pulled loose, and he looked again down the road where the little white cat still waited.

So, just around twilight, with supper already finished, and while Papa was inside the house watching television, and while Brother stood guard in the front driveway, Jordan took a slice of sandwich meat and a bottle of tap water and hurried down to the woods at the end of the road.

She called softly, "Here kitty, here kitty."

The cat had moved and sat just off the sand in the woods. Jordan squatted down and held out her hand with the meat. "Here, kitty kitty kitty," she called again. It stood and moved a little closer.

"Want me to put it in your bowl?" Jordan asked. "Come on."

The cat followed to the log and Jordan filled the water bowl and tore up the meat into the other bowl and the cat began to purr and lick Jordan's hand and eat the food as she tore . . . a warm scratchy little tongue licking Jordan's hand.

Jordan sat on the log. The colors deepened, and the scent of sweet olive filled the air, and Jordan watched the white cat eat from the bowl.

"You are such a good sweet cat," Jordan said quietly into the still.

The cat gobbled down the rest of the meat and purred loudly, letting Jordan pet its head.

"Brother wanted to come, too," Jordan said. "But Papa is home. Brother says hey."

It was getting hard to see. The patches of sand in the brightening moonlight took on a look of snowdrifts against the dark leaves and straw covering the earth. Shadows darkened and blurred into each other.

Papa would soon be calling them inside.

Jordan stood up. "I have to go," she said. The cat followed. Jordan stopped.

"You *can't* come." She picked it up and put it in the woods off the road. "Now you stay out of the way of people," she said sternly and hurried toward home. Lights were on in the big house and dotted windows way across the river and marshes.

On the other side of the road, it was dark in the rental. Dark and lonely. Jordan always felt happy when people would come there.

And past the wooded lot was Brother, waving excitedly in the end of the drive and pointing. Jordan stopped, thinking Papa must be able to see if she came beyond the trees. But Brother pointed to her and then she saw. The cat had followed.

"No," Jordan said. She picked up a stick, throwing it down in front of the cat. "Go back. *Go . . . back!*" She picked up another stick and the cat went into the woods.

Jordan went and stood frowning by Brother. They watched the road. "It's learning not to follow," Jordan said. "It's a smart cat."

A breeze picked up and rustled the leaves and clouds began to roll in from the sea and cover the moon.

"Did it like the food?" Brother asked.

"It loved the food. It wanted more. And it remembers us. It really likes us."

"Did you say I said 'Hey'?"

Jordan nodded. "I remembered," she said.

They glanced toward the house. Papa had turned on a light in the kitchen. The roof looked black against the deep blue of the sky. The oak limbs hung low.

Rumblings came from the clouds and Jordan and Brother stood in the dark and thought that now the white cat was almost their very own cat.

Chapter 42

WHEN JORDAN AND Brother got home from school the next day, the man from the creek was there. The man with the high cheekbones. The man who had looked familiar. He was there at the house with Papa. Jordan and Brother stood staring at the man as they entered the house, surprised.

"Well, don't jus' stand there lookin' fool," Papa said. "Ain't they a pair?" he snickered. The man stared. Jordan felt her face grow hot.

"G'on," Papa said. "Do y' homework."

Jordan and Brother went to the kitchen. Papa would not check to see they had done their homework. They got some pretzels and sat on the back steps eating and listening to the murmur of Papa and the man talking in the house. When they finished eating, they walked back through the path to the river and out on the old dock.

They looked across the shining water, across the green of the marsh beyond the river on the other side, to a cluster of condominiums nestled in trees on a small island.

"Looks like castles to me," Jordan said. A road had been built up in the marsh, providing access to the condominiums. A shiny dark-green car glided silently down the road and stopped momentarily at the gate, then moved beyond, vanishing in the trees.

"Mansions," Brother said, squinting across the wide expanse. Squinting to try to see clearer. The sun was low and off to the side. "Those people live in mansions."

"No, castles," Jordan said. "It's castles." She sat down on the edge of the dock. Brother sat beside her. They swung their legs. A snowy egret rose from the castles and spread its wings, gliding out toward the marshes beyond the condominium island. From where they saw it, it was tiny, but a dazzling white as the late sun caught its wings. They watched until it dipped again into the grasses far away.

"Do you think Papa doesn't like us?" Brother asked.

"We're his kids," Jordan said. "He likes us." She paused and frowned. "But sometimes he doesn't like us, too."

"Like when he's mad," Brother said.

"Yeah," Jordan said.

Jordan and Brother thought of when they came in from school. And Papa put them down. And Papa wasn't mad then. They knitted their brows and wondered. It was like some kids at school. But it was Papa.

The sun dropped lower and the sky glowed stained-glass pink.

Jordan turned and looked for the white cat. She sensed it was there, just out of sight, watching with its jewel-green eyes.

Chapter 43

THE MAN WAS STILL there when they went back, thinking it would soon be suppertime. His name was Jim. He stayed for supper.

Jim brought the television to the kitchen counter and Jordan noticed he kept an eye on it the whole time they ate.

Papa made burgers. Brother stayed far away from the stove as Papa cooked, hovering against the far wall. Papa had put Brother's hand in boiling water once, to teach him a lesson. It was the first time the social workers had come. And Jordan and Brother had learned not to go to school and say anything.

Not even ask for Band-Aids and that pink medicine that some of the kids got from the nurse for itches and stuff. Not even to ask for that.

Jordan thought it would be kind of fun to have company for supper, but she started to say something while the local news was on and Papa yelled at her to shut up. Jordan felt her face turning red. It was the second time Papa had embarrassed her in front of Jim.

And after the news went off Jordan listened to Papa and Jim talk about a clerk in a robbery, held up by two men hidden in dark clothes and ski masks. She listened to Papa and Jim call the man a name and call the police fools and she listened to them laugh.

It was like Papa and the animals. Like doing the wrong thing was funny and someone had been shot in the hold up. It wasn't funny. Jordan looked at them, puzzled. Papa caught her look. She quickly looked back at her plate.

"You got somethin' you wanna say?" Papa threw the words at her. Jordan kept her head down and stared at her plate.

"No," she answered.

Papa let it go. Jim and Papa got beers and went back to the living room. And after that Papa decided they watched too much television. So Jordan and Brother didn't watch. When Papa was home, Papa watched, and once when Papa wasn't there, Brother turned it on, but it wouldn't work. Something Papa did in the fuse box. And Jordan scolded Brother and wiped off the knob, like Papa would go and find out they tried to work it.

Maybe Jordan should have known then. Maybe she did know in a way, but didn't want to know. Or maybe Jordan was just trying too hard not to think about Papa. About the way Papa put them down. About the way Papa hadn't told them right about Mama. About the animals. About fear.

One time Jordan saw a snake in the grasses back of the house, and then it slipped out of sight. She wasn't sure what it could do or would do, but it was there. Under the cover of the grasses and plants. It lived there.

Chapter 44

ONE AFTERNOON WHEN the sky was blue-black with thunderheads over the city and the air was cool with the oncoming rain and when there was a still quiet, Jordan crawled through the rabbit runs and into the little hollow under the bush.

Jim had come over and Jordan didn't like to be around Jim. Not after Papa had put her down in front of him before, and then yelled at her at the table, too. So Jordan waited in her hideout, smelling the earth and the old leaves, the air cool on her face.

She picked up the conch shell and ran her fingers over its surface. She put it to her ear. Was it the ocean from a hundred years ago that she heard? Trapped in there for a hundred years?

The call of a single bird floated above her.

Jordan froze. Jim and Papa were in the backyard. She could hear them talking. Familiar words. All-night store, dumb clerk, ski masks. Papa laughed. ". . . good money fast . . . ," he said. And Jim said something about "another store." Saturday? Did he say Saturday?

Why were Papa and Jim talking about ski masks and all-night stores again? It sounded like Papa thought it was good . . . to get money that way . . . and Jim . . . it almost sounded like Jim . . . Did Jim rob that store?

Did . . . Papa?

Jordan waited there, hidden by the brambles, and they left.

She sat on her knees and put the old conch shell back on the earth and looked at it lie there in that cool light. Just looked at it while a dove rustled nearby in the fallen leaves and Jordan watched the dove until it disappeared in the brush and then she let herself think of something tucked under Papa's sweatshirt and carried into the night. And she thought of Papa saying it was early, when it was not early, after the bar and grill, like he wanted them to remember it as early when they got home. And Jordan thought of the robbery on the local news and her papa and Jim laughing at the way you could not tell who the two men on the videotape were, about the tax money and the real estate man.

About how someone got shot in that robbery on the television and about the animals and about the way Papa didn't care.

A crackling of thunder, closer now, and the metallic smell of rain. Jordan crawled out of the hideout on her knees and back through the little tunnel in the branches.

In the house Brother waited at the back screen door. It was dark inside, and the rain began splatting on the windows, dripping through the roof over the kitchen. Papa had tried to fix that spot up on the roof. He would be angry when he saw it had not worked. Jordan pulled the little stained rug over to the wet spot to wipe it up and Brother got out the pan and set it on the floor to catch the drops, and after looking out the front window to make sure Papa's car was gone, Jordan told Brother what she heard back of their house in the underbrush in her hideout.

They stood at the back door and watched the rain come down and watched the yard fill up with pools of water and the sky change from blue and black to gray as the storm moved on out toward the sea and only the rain was left to fill up their yard and leak through their roof.

"The law would want to know," Jordan said, putting a finger on a drop on the screen and drawing it down to make a line of tiny water-filled squares.

"But it would be wrong to tell on your papa," Brother said.

"Yes," agreed Jordan. "It would be wrong to get your papa in trouble with the law."

They listened to the soft rain sounds, to rain spilling over in a puddle from the roof. "We can't really be sure," Jordan said.

"And Papa would be real mad at us," Brother said. "He would be madder than ever, wouldn't he?"

It was true. If they said anything, then, when the law left, Papa would be really mad. They would have done something awful bad. It would be the worst thing they ever did.

They went to the window in their room and blew on it, making frosty patches.

"Someone was shot," Jordan said.

Brother drew in his frosty patch with his finger. A face. A face without a mouth. "Were they killed?" Brother asked.

Jordan looked at Brother. "I don't remember. Maybe not. I hope not."

They heard a car and turned, drawing in quick breaths, but it went on by.

Jordan blew on the window again and drew raindrops in the frost. She whispered, "What if someone else would get shot because we didn't tell?"

Brother squinted at her drawing. He moved to another window and blew. Jordan came and joined him. "What if?" she asked again.

"What if Papa didn't do it?" Brother said.

They drew more pictures. Jordan drew a cat. And a possum. And they went back to the kitchen and sat in the gray light and were filled with an uneasy sense of what they knew and what they did not know.

Chapter 45

IN THE MORNING JORDAN and Brother missed the school bus, and Papa went to grab something at the store. They wouldn't miss anything important at school this late in the year anyway, Papa said.

Jordan and Brother carried sand in cups from the rental house driveway. They sat in their drive making little hills out of the sand.

They said nothing about yesterday. Nothing at all.

But what if people found out?

Brother had some tiny cars Mama brought him one time. He pushed his fingers through the sand making tracks for roads and sounds for the cars that he pulled, one by one, out of his pockets.

A bird hopped on an old split-log bench under the tangled wisteria vines growing by the side of the yard. Brother looked up and scrunched his face in the sun. A car with a boat on a trailer parked across the road. Something about it, about the slant of the sun or the boat perhaps, something, made Jordan remember walking to the ocean with Mama and Brother years ago, and the stories of the man with the boat named *Shell Dancer,* and the inlet. And the lighthouse. And Mama in a dress that was pale-blue stripes on white.

"Are they coming to rent the house?" Brother asked.

"Maybe," Jordan said. She tilted her head and stared, too, at the people in the car.

"They're watching us." Brother frowned. He pushed one of the cars deep into the sand hill and looked at his fingers covered partway. "Do you think they know we took the sand?"

A car whirred by and it was quiet again.

Across the road a man and a woman got out of the car. The man stood with his hands on his back stretching a bit, tired from sitting a long time, and Jordan watched. When the couple started across the road, Jordan jumped to her feet. "Look Brother! It's *them!*"

Uncle Bob and Aunt Viv laughed. Aunt Viv gave Jordan a hug. "My goodness, you two have grown!" she said, looking them over approvingly. "Look how much they have grown, Bob. How long has it been? Four years? Five?"

Jordan grinned. "We sent you a card."

"That was some pretty card, too," Uncle Bob said, and smiled. His wrinkled face crinkled and the sun blazed off his white hair.

He looked around at Brother still sitting in the shade of the live oak, stuffing his cars into his pockets. "Hey there, Carson."

"Hey," Brother said.

"I couldn't find you all in the phone book," Uncle Bob said. "I was going to call before we came."

"Phone's cut off sometimes," Jordan said.

"We saw your mama."

Brother got up, moving closer.

"She's back down here," Uncle Bob continued. "Did your daddy tell you?"

Jordan shook her head no.

"Should've," Uncle Bob said. "Caseworker told him."

"Now, Bob," Aunt Viv said. "The good news is she's better. She's got new pills. All she can talk about is when she can see you two."

Jordan and Brother looked at each other, their faces bright.

"When you wrote . . . we hadn't known 'bout your mama." Uncle Bob hesitated. "From time to time I sent letters . . . asking how y'all were doing." He looked at the house. "Never heard anything back though. Figured . . . " Uncle Bob looked back at the children. "Well, I figured wrong. And I sure was glad to get that pretty card."

Jordan and Brother grinned.

"We wanted to come pay a visit," Uncle Bob said. He looked around the yard with a frown.

"Is your daddy 'round?"

"No," Jordan said.

"Well look," Aunt Viv said, "we brought the boat

along. We thought you two might like to go out on the boat with us."

Jordan and Brother beamed at each other. "We *would*!" Jordan said.

"When you think your daddy's coming back?" Uncle Bob asked.

"He's gone to the store . . . but he'll be back soon." Jordan wished she could say when. She wished the yard didn't have all Papa's junk in it. She wished Uncle Bob could be pleased with the way they were keeping up his brother's house.

Brother eyed the boat across the street hungrily.

"You like that boat?" Uncle Bob asked, and laughed.

Brother nodded eagerly.

"We'll be back later then, when your daddy gets back," Uncle Bob said. "All right?"

Jordan nodded.

She and Brother stood in the yard. They watched Uncle Bob and Aunt Viv get in the car. The sun filtered through the oak tree and speckled their faces with light.

Brother pushed his glasses up on his nose. "Will they come back, Jordan?"

Jordan studied the old man buckling his seat belt. The air was warm and still.

"It's hot. They're tired now. They'll go get something for lunch." Jordan dusted her hands off on her jeans, and combed at her hair with her fingers. "After lunch, then they'll be back."

The car rolled off and turned down a side road and they waved as Aunt Viv lifted a hand and smiled from her window. Shadow patterns slid along the car door and the white sides of the boat and then the words painted on the back of the boat. Shadows and sunlight across neat black letters on the back of the boat just before it slipped behind the trees and left Jordan standing surprised at the edge of her yard.

Shell Dancer II.

"The lighthouse man," Jordan said.

Chapter 46

U NCLE BOB AND AUNT Viv did come back and
Papa talked to them in the front yard. He
tapped his fingers on the roof of his car, and
said Jordan and Brother could go with them for a ride on
the river, but he had things to do.

Jordan studied his eyes. Was he mad?

Or something else?

"Behave yourselves," Papa said, and he got into his
car.

So Jordan and Brother rode in the back seat of Uncle
Bob's car to the boat landing and watched him back the
boat down the ramp to get it in the water. They put on
life jackets and climbed into the bobbing boat.

"Everybody hold on," Uncle Bob said as he drove
out into the river. Jordan and Brother laughed and
squealed in the boat as they flew along through the racing wind across the choppy gray-green water and saw
the river and the marshes, the mansions and the castles,
the bridge and the dock out back of their own house, all
from Uncle Bob's boat on the river itself.

The river narrowed to a creek in the marsh, and they rode on until the water joined the ocean at the inlet, and the lighthouse rose out of the waves, cut off from a wild island beyond, by the sea, some fifty years ago.

Uncle Bob brought the boat to a stop and turned off the motor. "Look at that old lighthouse," he said. "Now that's a pretty thing."

The water tipped them side to side, making splashing sounds as little waves hit the boat. Jordan lifted her chin high. She studied the top of the old building. A round room of windows. The wind from the ocean cooled her.

"Mama used to tell us about you," Jordan said. "Mama said one time . . . when we were little . . . she said she saw you at the post office."

Uncle Bob shook his head. "It couldn't have been me, Jordan."

Jordan knew that. It was just a stranger Mama saw that time at the post office. Not the man with the boat. Not Uncle Bob. Jordan knew that now.

She looked back at Uncle Bob.

"But you remember coming here with Mama when she was a little girl," Jordan said.

Uncle Bob smiled. He squinted toward the lighthouse and the island past it. No one lived there. It was just sand dunes and sweet myrtles . . . other plants . . . birds. . . .

"Your mama was just a little thing then," he said.

"And I knew my way all around these waters. Nothing but oyster beds and mudflats some places out there. But I knew how to get through. We'd collect shells out there. . . . Just beyond the lighthouse . . . over on that beach."

Jordan watched a line of pelicans gliding by. She looked back at Uncle Bob.

"And as I recall," Uncle Bob said, "your mama sure did like that old lighthouse."

Jordan smiled. "Yeah, she did."

Uncle Bob and Aunt Viv stayed three more days. Papa had little to say to them or the children. Uncle Bob and Aunt Viv rented a house and, every day after school, Jordan and Brother went with them for walks on the pier and out in the boat.

Jordan did not forget the white cat. Near sunset she would run through the woods to the dirt road with what food she could get. Some days she saw the white cat. Most days she just left the food. She never stayed long now.

Now she'd heard Papa and Jim.

Now Papa was so silent.

On their last day there, Uncle Bob and Aunt Viv took Jordan and Brother and Papa to supper in the little old sidewalk restaurant two blocks from the ocean.

When Uncle Bob and Aunt Viv left them at their house, Jordan and Brother charged through the path to the old dock over the marsh. They could see the bridge from there. They could wave when Uncle Bob and Aunt Viv's car with its lights on in the fast fading dusk, and with the *Shell Dancer II* following right behind, headed out across the river for the long drive back upstate.

Chapter 47

THE WHITE CAT WAITED in the trees. It was cool, and the sun was just beginning to dry the dew from the night, glittering on the long rippled leaves of the ferns. There was time after breakfast, Jordan had thought, to take some food to the white cat. Time before Papa wanted them to help him in the yard. She found the cat waiting near the log and it came to its bowl when she called.

Jordan thought she had taught it not to follow her home, and when Jordan went that morning early and fed it, she told it again to stay. She told it not to follow.

The cat did not learn.

It trailed from a distance, a ripple in the grass, small and unseen, so when Jordan looked back, it was not there for her to see.

Chapter 48

THAT MORNING, FULL of blues and greens and yellows, Jordan and Brother and Papa wrapped wire around a large wooden spool out back of the house.

And the white cat came.

Jordan's heart sunk. "Go 'way!" she yelled, but the little thing kept on coming.

"Let it come," Papa said as Jordan picked up a stick.

"Hey, pretty cat." Brother leaned to pet it on its head. It rubbed against him and purred loudly.

Jordan looked at Papa. He stood eyeing the boy and the cat. She had seen the look before. With the possum on the road.

"Go 'way!" she yelled again, moving toward the cat, but Papa caught her shoulder and slung her back. She stumbled and tripped, and Papa reached down and pulled the cat up by the scruff of its neck.

It hissed and wriggled, its legs flailing and back feet kicking. Papa dropped it and in the same movement kicked it to the grass. The scream was terrible. The cat stumbled back to its feet, fell, got up again and limped off into the bushes and Jordan looked back at Papa's face.

He laughed. "Told it not to come back. Maybe now it'll listen," he said.

Jordan looked around. Brother was crying. Staring after the little cat. Staring at the place it had gone into the woods.

Suddenly Jordan screamed at Papa. "That cat was coming to *me!*" she screamed. Her face was red. She wiped away the tears. *"You knew!"* But Papa was already disappearing into the house. He did not look back.

Jordan had never yelled like that at Papa. You did not yell like that at Papa.

Jordan and Brother stood in the yard and the chirring of insects surrounded them. Jordan would not let Papa hear her screams anymore.

Jordan and Brother looked for the cat.

They looked under the tangles of vines where it had disappeared. They crept through the woods and Jordan called "Here kitty kitty!" until they came to the big house on pilings beyond the woods. They hoped the people there would find it and help it. They looked down the dirt road. They couldn't find the white cat. They hoped it would be all right, that it would stop hurting and heal.

But she knew the little cat would never be the same even if its body did heal.

And maybe . . . maybe . . . yes, she wished it would find some other girl and boy to care for it . . . so it would never be near Papa again.

Chapter 49

RAIN CAME THAT NIGHT and left pools of water in the road. The water was clear and dark, and trees and sky were mirrored there.

In the morning, Jordan found the pools at the end of the drive. There were gardens in pools like these, Mama used to say. Just right there in the middle of the street. Gardens.

Jordan waited there, under the palmettos out by the road, looking deep in the rain pools, in Mama's cool watery gardens, until Papa left in the car, just like Jordan had figured he would.

Then Jordan walked the few blocks to Center Street. She knew where the island police building was, and she went in and sat waiting in her best dress, figuring she had better look serious. She smoothed it over her knees and wished she had taken it to the Laundromat more recently.

A lady in the hall had told Jordan where to wait, told her a policeman would be there in just a minute. But this was more than a minute. She was sure.

She did not have time to wait around.

Perhaps it was a good thing that a policeman was not there because maybe she should leave.

Because maybe she could not tell the police about the robberies . . . about Papa and the robberies.

A man came in the door then. Jordan stared at the uniform, and her heart beat harder. A policeman. He smiled her way and went to the desk and was talking to someone and maybe she could get out of here now and if she ran fast they would not be able to catch her and ask her what she was doing coming in there and wasting the taxpayers' money playing games with the police.

And then they could not tell Papa that she had been there.

Papa was never supposed to know.

"What can I do for you, young lady?" the officer asked.

He was talking to her, but she could not talk.

The officer sat down beside her. He seemed friendly enough. "You got something you want to tell me?" he asked.

Jordan pushed her hair back. She wished she had one of those hair things that held your hair neat. She felt like she could not get enough air. She could leave.

But then, she really did not want to leave.

"I know where there's maybe gonna be a robbery," Jordan said. After she spoke those words, it was easier. Even the part about who might be doing the robbery.

Papa. Papa who did not care one thing about kicking her little stray white cat.

"I heard my papa and Jim talking. It sounded like they said . . . like they said . . . another store this Saturday," she said. "That's today."

Jordan took a deep breath. She had done what she came to do. She was not sorry. She did not want to think any more about what she had just done.

She looked at the officer. "You promise not to tell on me?"

"I won't tell," he said.

"And I can go now?"

He smiled. "You run on. Someone will check this out."

Jordan dashed out to the hallway and ran, glad he didn't make her waste time waiting around, glad it was over. She ran, and the sound of her feet echoed in the empty hall.

Chapter 50

OUTSIDE THE SUN was warm and bright, and Jordan started toward home quickly, walking past a boiled peanut stand in a vacant lot, wishing she had some money to buy a bag and take it home for her and Brother to eat on the back porch.

"Get over here!"

She did not hear the angry voice until it came again. Was that Papa's voice? Papa wasn't supposed to be here!

Jordan looked up. She ran to the car and pulled on the door, climbed into the back seat, sank into the corner, dug her hand into the rip in the upholstery. Her breath came quick and shallow. The car stopped in front of the ocean grocery on the corner. Papa got out and Jordan sat in the hot car and little trickles of sweat rolled down from under her knees to her socks.

Papa was never supposed to know.

Why did he have to come by in this car?

Jordan waited. The hot dusty car smell got stronger. The quiet deeper. And even the blond boy walking right outside with his surfboard seemed farther away.

Did Papa see her come out of the police building? If he guessed what she had said in there, then he and Jim would not go.

Then the police would think she was a liar and they might break their promise to her not to tell Papa, if it looked like she was a liar.

Liar. Liar. What did you think you were doing . . . lying like that about your own papa? Jordan scrunched her eyes shut. It was what people would say.

Except Papa. Papa would know she did not lie.

And then he was back in the car and they were riding to the house and she was so hot, but she dared not try to open the window now.

"The teacher told us—"

"Shut your mouth till I'm ready to talk to you!"

He slammed the car door. Jordan followed him in the house. Papa put the bag from the grocery on the kitchen table. Jordan stood at the front door and Brother waited outside the screen.

Papa came back. His voice was quiet and mocking. "Go ahead. Explain what you were doing. I'd like to hear it."

"The teacher told us . . . "—Jordan tried to swallow. Her mouth was sticky dry—"to get a book to read from the library. And after you went, then I remembered."

"Where's the book?"

Jordan shook her head. "They weren't open."

"Then how come, Miss Liar, I find you way down past the library?"

Jordan hung her head . . . pulling at her hair, pulling it down along her cheek.

"I asked you a question!" he shouted.

"I wanted to see the ocean . . . but I didn't . . . I came back."

Papa watched her. He stood there and watched her.

"You think you getting mighty big for your britches, don't you?"

Jordan stared at the floor.

"Don't you!"

"No, sir."

Papa's voice was quiet again, taunting. He took his time. "You lie . . . you did lie, didn't you? You disobey and leave this house and go off down Center Street. . . ."

Out of the corner of her eye Jordan could see Brother still outside the door, his hands up on his ears, waiting for it to be over.

"When I get back, I'm gonna take care of you," Papa said. "You hear me?"

Jordan stared at his feet and nodded.

"But don't you think you're gonna be out playing all day. You've had your fun, young lady."

If he would just leave. Leave. And get back so late he'd've forgotten all this.

"You got some school books?"

"Yes, sir."

"You wanted to study so hard. Get in your room and read 'em."

Jordan ran to her room. The light was grayed. She waited by the door. She heard him leaving, saying something to Brother.

She got her book and the bed creaked as she sat on the edge looking at a picture in the front, a white building lit up at night, and thinking it must be one of the alabaster cities from the song at school. She sat in the quiet looking at the picture.

She knew Papa was gone now, but she did not close the book. She had better keep the book out.

She curled up on the bed, feeling the soft impressions of the old spread on her face. Someone was hammering, building a house, a street or two over. Brother came outside the bedroom window asking her when she was coming out.

"Not yet," she said and he left. She listened for almost an hour until little patterns from the spread covered her cheek and Brother came to the window again and she decided it was safe enough now to leave the room and go outside with Brother.

Chapter 51

THAT NIGHT PAPA came back for supper and Jordan fixed frozen pizzas and was as good as she knew how and Papa had lost interest in giving her the beating for this morning and he left, just as he was supposed to, according to the plan.

She watched the door after he left for a long time, the dingy, gray-white, shadowy door with a bright little brassy light reflected in the knob. And she wondered why she took this chance. But of course she knew. It was the cat. She took the chance for the white cat.

She listened to the scratchy sounds of Brother's cars as he played on the floor and was afraid for headlights in the drive. Afraid, no matter whose car they would turn out to be. But for now, there were no lights in the driveway.

She fell asleep on the back porch in the cool under a moon-blue sky. She fell asleep not knowing if Papa would come back through that door, out of the night, like he always had before.

Chapter 52

IT HAD BEEN FIVE DAYS since that night. Five days in the foster home. Five days and Brother had not talked to anyone except to whisper to Jordan.

Papa had not come home.

It was the last week of school before summer now, and Jordan had packed her book bag, and gone to the schoolyard to stand by the fence with the late-bus girls.

"Is that your mama that drives you to school now?" one of the girls asked Jordan. "Someone told me that was your mama."

"That's the foster mama," Jordan said. "We're there temporary."

After all, they couldn't stay there. If they stayed there, then who would look after the white cat?

"Is your foster mama mean?" another girl asked.

The foster mama was nice enough, Jordan thought. Her name was Mrs. Green and she was okay, except for making them work too hard on homework.

"She's not real mean," Jordan said. "But we're not going to stay there."

Jordan did not really know that. The social worker couldn't tell her how long they would stay there. "Maybe a long time," the foster mama had said. "We'd like to have you stay with us."

Jordan did not want to stay in the foster home. She didn't know what she had expected though . . . if a girl went and told the police what she had about Papa.

And Jordan wondered. Would she ever tell anyone it was her that told on Papa?

Jordan picked an oleander off the bush by the fence and examined it. Oleander was poison, wasn't it? She dropped it and rubbed her fingers on her skirt to get the poison off.

And had she thought Mama would suddenly get well from the brain disorder and come home? Is that what she had thought?

"Did your parents put you there?"

"No," Jordan said. "We just had to go there for a while, that's all."

She didn't say a social worker came in the middle of the night and found them asleep on the back porch and told them they had to go to the foster home. Told them Papa was in jail. Had them pack up their stuff in black plastic trash bags. And leave. Right there in the middle of the night. Leave their home. And Papa in jail. She didn't say that.

The girls saw their bus and ran off to get in line. Jordan watched them go. At least that wasn't her old bus.

She didn't like to see her old bus ride off toward her island without her. She didn't like to think about the little house sitting there empty.

Jordan went to wait under the live oak with Brother. He played there after school until the foster mama came to get them. It was cool and shady. Rain had swept away the sandy soil below the roots on one side, leaving step-like places to sit.

"You need to talk to the foster mama," Jordan said. "You need to talk to the other kids at the house, too."

"Do they know Papa's in jail?" Brother asked.

"Don't know," Jordan said. There were three other kids. It was kind of crowded. "Maybe they've got parents in jail, too," she said.

"I don't like it there, and they don't like me." Brother knelt on the ground and pushed his toy car into a little cave under a root. "When's Papa gonna come get us? Do we have to stay there always?"

Jordan didn't know. She ran her fingers in the sand leaving wavy lines, and looked up through the branches at the blue sky. The river would be blue now. Maybe high tide. High tide spilling blue all out in the marsh grasses as well. And maybe the white cat was sunning back on the dock like when she first saw it.

Maybe it came there looking for her. And she wasn't there.

Jordan wanted to go home.

Chapter 53

SUMMER CAME. PAPA didn't come for them, but Uncle Bob and Aunt Viv did. A little over a week after Jordan and Brother went to the foster home, Uncle Bob and Aunt Viv came.

They brought their boat and their suitcases and went to see the social service people who had tracked them down. And they went to see the police and they took Jordan and Brother away from the foster home and back to the island.

Somehow Jordan had known they would come . . . had known Mama's lighthouse man would come.

In the hushed light of late afternoon Jordan and Brother walked down the grayed wooden steps to the beach. They heard Uncle Bob and Aunt Viv behind them standing on the boardwalk over the dunes, talking of U-Haul-Its and what they wanted to bring down here and watching the waves and the gulls that stood in groups all facing the wind.

Jordan and Brother went to the water's edge. Their

feet sank in the soft sand of a beach fluffed by tides and wind.

"Will Uncle Bob and Aunt Viv stay long?" Brother asked.

"They're gonna stay for good," Jordan said.

Brother squinted into the wind. "Even after Papa gets out? Will we stay with them then?"

"Even then," Jordan said.

The wind, strong from building over miles of open sea, surrounded them and flapped their clothes. "What about the white cat, Jordie?" Brother asked.

Jordan looked out to the lights illuminating the white sides of the shrimp boats above the gray of the sea. "We'll look for the white cat," she answered.

The salty, foaming water of the Atlantic curled about her bare feet and tumbled up to her ankles. The shrimp boats became floating stars that dotted the edge of the sea. And she stood there until Aunt Viv called to them saying it was time to go home for supper.

Chapter 54

SUMMER WENT ON. Weeks passed. Uncle Bob and Aunt Viv took Jordan and Brother a hundred fifty miles to see their house in Mont Clare, out in the country, up in the rolling sand hills. They got things to bring back to the island. And every day Aunt Viv called the animal shelters to see if they'd found a white cat.

"Can we go look now?" Jordan asked. "Can we take food?"

Aunt Viv didn't mind. She liked cats. So the children took bits of food and searched for the cat down the dirt road every day, and though Jordan called, and they left food and water, and sometimes Uncle Bob even drove them slow around the island looking, they did not see the white cat.

For a few days, Uncle Bob had wandered about the house and the yard shaking his head, muttering to himself, until one day he took Brother and Jordan to town and they bought tools and paint for the house.

Uncle Bob hired someone to help fix the yard and replace the old boards on the dock. It felt strong under

Jordan's feet and she didn't even know, until then, until that new dock, how weak the old one had been. Jordan stood there over the marsh with Uncle Bob.

"Next summer all those posts'll have boards between 'em. It'll stretch all the way out to the river," Uncle Bob said.

"Like when Grandpa lived here," Jordan said. She stared down through the open spaces between the planks into the marsh water and folded her arms tightly.

"Why can't Mama come see it now?" she asked.

Uncle Bob put his hands in his pockets. "She's not ready, is what her caseworker says." He looked at Jordan. "She'll come see you again."

Jordan studied his face.

"She will," Uncle Bob said. "In the meantime, you could go see her. Go see where she lives. A little visit."

Jordan dropped her arms to her side and moved close to Uncle Bob. "Mama'll like the new dock, won't she?" she said.

Uncle Bob put his hand on her shoulder. "You bet."

Wood storks rose from grasses out in the marsh. Jordan watched them, watched their powerful wings lift them higher and higher and higher above the river . . . and higher still into the blue above her, on upward currents they soared.

Chapter 55

ONE EVENING, AFTER supper, when the island seemed to be resting and colored in shades of blue, Brother came and sat by Jordan out the front door.

"What's it like where Mama lives?" Brother asked. "Is it a bad place?"

"Uncle Bob says it's not bad at all."

"Papa didn't want us to go there."

"I'm going," Jordan said.

She looked at Brother. "You'll have to decide for you." She looked back across the road. A light was on in the rental.

Brother knitted his brow. "What about Papa? Are you going to see Papa?"

Jordan didn't want to see Papa. She pushed her hair back and it felt silky and clean and it still surprised her to feel it that way. What would Papa think of her now? And Brother in his clean new jeans and T-shirt, the new glasses and haircut. What would Papa think of the two of them now?

She frowned. It was hard to think about Papa.

Did Papa know it was her who had told the law?

"I don't know about Papa," Jordan said quietly. They looked at each other. There was time.

They sat in the light that spilled out the front door and down to the yard. The summer air moved about them, and Jordan pointed to the tall grasses across the road.

"Look . . . the white cat . . . ," she whispered.

The shape glided under the yard lamp, and became white. The cat stood and turned her head looking at them for a minute, then tripped across the driveway and into the shadows, into some secret pathway, some safe place.

"Will she come back?" Brother asked.

Jordan thought she saw the silvery shape just off in the brambles.

"She'll come back. I know she will. Maybe even tonight," Jordan said.

They sat on the front steps and listened to crickets, and to the sounds of cars coming and going down on Center Street. They waited for their cat and listened and the small clear sound of a mockingbird came from way down the dirt road in the white cat's woods. They sat there and waited because their cat was almost home.